Dear America

The Diary
of Minnie Bonner

A CITY TOSSED
AND BROKEN

JUDY BLUNDELL

SCHOLASTIC INC. • NEW YORK

Copyright © 2013 by Judy Blundell

All rights reserved. Published by Scholastic Inc., *Publishers since 1920.*
SCHOLASTIC, DEAR AMERICA, and associated logos are trademarks and/or registered
trademarks of Scholastic Inc. No part of this publication may be reproduced,
stored in a retrieval system, or transmitted in any form or by any means,
electronic, mechanical, photocopying, recording, or otherwise, without written
permission of the publisher. For information regarding permission, write to
Scholastic Inc., Attention: Permissions Department,
557 Broadway, New York, NY 10012.

Library of Congress Cataloging-in-Publication Data

Blundell, Judy.
A city tossed and broken : the diary of Minnie Bonner / Judy Blundell. — 1st ed.
p. cm. — (Dear America)
Summary: It is 1906, and when her family is cheated out of their tavern,
fourteen-year-old Minnie Bonner is forced to become a maid to the Sump family,
who are moving to San Francisco — three weeks before the great earthquake.
ISBN 978-0-545-31022-2 (paper over board)
[1. San Francisco Earthquake and Fire, Calif., 1906 — Fiction. 2. Earthquakes
— Fiction. 3. Household employees — Fiction. 4. Family life — California —
Fiction. 5. Diaries — Fiction. 6. San Francisco (Calif.) — History — 20th century
— Fiction.] I. Title. II. Series: Dear America.
PZ7.B627146Cit 2013
813.6 — dc23
2012014742

10 9 8 7 6 5 4 3 2 1   13 14 15 16 17

The text type was set in ITC Legacy Serif.
The display type was set in P22 Arts and Crafts Hunter.
Book design by Kevin Callahan
Photo research by Amla Sanghvi

Printed in the U.S.A. 23
First edition, March 2013

PHILADELPHIA,
PENNSYLVANIA

1906

MARCH 30, 1906

I want to say at the very start that I am not the type to do this. Write my feelings down, I mean. We are talkers in my family. If I'm sad or happy or confused, I say it. But suddenly I am finding that nobody is saying anything at all.

You would think, diary, that when your family loses everything, you'd want to talk it over. Wouldn't you?

How can your whole life change so quickly, so all-of-a-sudden?

Mama just sits and stares, or says, *Not now, Minnie. I'm trying to think.*

And Papa is just gone.

Now here is a word I would like to have heard from him. *Good-bye.*

Now I will record what happened today.

All I knew was that the grand lady, Mrs. Chester Sump, was coming to call on Mama with her daughter, Lily. This required both of us to be wearing our best dresses and for me to wash the good tea set and bring it downstairs to the tavern.

Mama and I made sandwiches on thin slices of bread — chicken salad, cheese and chutney, and deviled ham. I baked a chocolate cake.

It is so strange to see the tavern closed on a weekday.

Mrs. Sump didn't eat any of the sandwiches. She picked up the chicken, sniffed it, and put it down again. When Lily picked up the ham, Mrs. Sump looked at her and Lily put it down.

Mrs. Sump took a small bite of cake and put down her fork as though it wasn't up to her standards. But then you could see how hard it was for her not to eat it, because I make a delicious cake. In the end she ate two slices. She wouldn't let Mama cut any for Lily.

"Marriageable girls should not eat cake," she said.

Well, that is something I never heard before. All the more reason not to marry, I suppose.

Lily didn't seem to mind. She just looked on, a vacant expression on her face, as though gaslights were lit in an empty room. She had a round face and a sharp nose, but pretty green eyes. She ignored me, but I was not sitting at the table with them, I was fetching and carrying. I did not realize that I was auditioning for the role of maid until I listened at the kitchen door.

In the time it took for me to wash up, it was settled between them. No money changed hands, but I've been sold just the same.

"That's that, then," Mrs. Sump said to Mama. "I take the girl."

I pushed the swinging door just a crack so I could peer through the gap. The tavern was empty except for the table we'd set in the corner. Mama sat with her hands folded tightly. She had taken off her apron when Mrs. Sump came to the door. She looked so strange without it. Like any other mother in a dark gray dress with jet buttons. I only know her as the owner of a bustling tavern, always in an apron, usually with her hands full carrying a tray or balancing three plates of hot dishes or settling a bill, making change in two seconds flat and always a smile, even at a bad tip.

Mrs. Sump sat at the edge of her chair as if it would contaminate her hindquarters. Her coat was silk and velvet and her dress frothed beneath in layers of scallops and trimming. Her hat sailed on her head like a ship, ribbons flying like flags. She was someone used to being listened to. I could see she didn't like Mama's hesitation.

"You say she's done washing, and mending, and cleaning," Mrs. Sump said. "I keep a tidy house."

"She's a good girl," Mama said. "She can even cook. She made the cake," she added, and if I wasn't so mad at her, I'd admire the way she said it, so cool, but letting Mrs. Sump know that she'd gobbled up two thick slices and could have gone for a third.

Mrs. Sump's hat shuddered in indignation. "I have a cook, Mrs. Bonner. I also have a house-keeper, a butler, a groom, and a full staff of servants. I'm doing you a favor, taking your girl off your hands. You won't have her keep while she's away, either. If you put that into the pot, you'll see what a favor I'm doing you. She's young — fourteen, you say? — still, she's tall."

"She's a good worker, ma'am," Mama said. She just kept staring down at her hands. She would squeeze one hand, then the other.

All I've been hearing for the past two weeks is how kind Mr. Sump has been. How he made us a loan of money that we badly needed and so we signed over the tavern and now he is so sorry but he's moving all his businesses to California and has a partner there who is making him sell everything here. And so the tavern is gone, and my parents have no work.

And we have no home, because we live above the tavern.

He gave us as much time as he could to make other arrangements, Mama said last night. Truly? I said. A month is enough time to dismantle a life? It went so quickly! Now we have to be out within the week.

Mrs. Sump has a proposition for us, Mama told me this morning. Now it turns out it's for me to be a lady's maid for her daughter, Lily, out in San Francisco, where they are moving in less than two weeks.

"She'll have her duties as a parlormaid, too," Mrs. Sump said. "Of course, my housekeeper usually does the hiring, but I'm making an exception in this case so that you know your daughter will be going to a good house. I wanted to have a look at the girl. She seems suitable. I will take her on. Our life in San Francisco will be very different. We'll be moving in the best society. Not that we aren't now," she added quickly.

"I'm sure you're very kind." Mother pressed her index finger to the inner corner of her eye.

Papa said many people have a "tell." This means a gesture they make but they don't even realize they're doing it, especially when they're trying to hide something. Mama puts a finger there when she's trying not to cry.

"And she won't be grubbing around in a tavern," Mrs. Sump proclaimed. "I'd say this is a rather better life for her."

She said it like this — *rah-thuh bett-uh.*

Mama didn't answer this. I wanted to pound on the other side of the door. Our tavern had been in the Moore family for over a hundred years. Benjamin Franklin had hoisted an ale at our table. We weren't a fine restaurant, we were just the Blue Spruce Tavern on Spruce Street, and that was good enough for the neighborhood. Everyone got a welcome who came through the door.

"Mrs. Bonner," Mrs. Sump said impatiently. "Are you in agreement? Done?"

"Done," Mama said.

She should have said *Sold!* Because that's what she did.

I leave for San Francisco in ten days.

APRIL 1, 1906

I did not wake up this morning and find all this to be a great practical joke for April Fool. My father did not walk in the door, laughing and teasing and saying, "Of course you're not going to San Francisco, you silly thing!"

No. Instead I am mending what needs to be mended and Mama is packing her things.

Well, what is there to say. Everything we know is gone and soon I will be. I'm to "train" as a maid (train like a horse?) before we leave for San Francisco. Mama has found lodging in a rooming house by the river.

Mama says,

I can't help what is.

You're almost fifteen, you're practically grown now.

Just be a good girl and do what you're told.

I have no choice, Min!

It's hard not to talk to someone you live with. Even when — especially when! — you're so filled up with angry words. Silence doesn't come natural to our house. Usually I fall asleep to the sounds of laughing and talk from the tavern downstairs. And in our own rooms above we are always telling each other what needs to be done or what was done or what will be done tomorrow. And when Papa was here there was singing and jokes. Now there is nothing but silence.

Papa has always taken off from time to time, but this time he's gone for good, Mama says.

How does she know he's gone for good?

She won't say.

I'm to go to Mrs. Sump's house to learn how to be a maid and then I'll travel on the train with Mrs. Sump and Lily. Mr. Sump is already in San

Francisco, has been for the past year on and off. Except for when he was here, dining at the tavern. When he first came in we were excited, because he's very rich and we hoped he'd bring his friends. Well, he did, and something happened and then he had to loan Papa money and then called in the loan, but I'm supposed to be grateful and think he was kind.

I don't understand any of it.

Mr. Sump built some kind of a palace out there, on Nob Hill. So Mrs. Sump told Mama. The Sump Mansion, she called it. Phew.

I want to ask Mama what Papa will do, how he'll find her once she moves and I'm gone, but I don't. I know what she'll say: *Your father is not coming back.*

What about school? I asked her, and she said, *You're fourteen, you can leave school to go to work. Just keep up with your reading,* she said. *San Francisco has a library just like Philadelphia — it's a very grand city, you know. I want you to join the library as soon as you get there. That's the first place I want you to find.*

Shall I replace you with books, then? I wanted to say.

There are too many words inside, like a pot of water at a rolling boil.

That's why I'm writing this. When the tavern closed, Cook left behind the book he wrote his recipes in. I saw it there on the counter and picked it up, grease stains on the red leather cover and faded gilt letters: RECIPES. It was only a quarter full of recipes, the rest of the pages were blank. He had wound a string around it to keep it together and stuck a pencil right inside the twine.

You are my secret, diary. Here is where I can finally talk.

I am starting out on a life where I can't say anything anymore, anything of what I feel or think. I'm to be a maid, alone in a city thousands of miles away. Who will I say things to now, like,

Should I make us some tea?

What a funny hat that lady has on.

I miss Papa.

Writing things down will get them out and on a page and over with.

I hate her.

I hate Mrs. Sump.

I hate her fat husband.
I hate San Francisco.
I hate my father for leaving.

APRIL 2, 1906

Mama came in last evening as I was stirring the soup I was making us for our dinner. She put a suitcase on the chair. It was a present. It was scuffed, the brass cloudy and scratched, though you could see she had tried to rub it shiny.

I'd never had such a thing before. I'd never had need of it. Presents were books and oranges or a new shirtwaist on a birthday or Christmas.

"If I had another way, I would take it, Min," she said. And then she gripped the chair back and I could see her throat working, like she was swallowing an extra-big piece of roast. "I'll save every penny and get back on my feet. Then I'll send for you. I *will*, Min. It's just the two of us now, and we have to save ourselves."

I said, "What if Papa comes back?" And she laughed without any laugh inside the laughter. And then just like that she was crying.

I was so mad at her for crying I just kept stirring the soup. After a minute she walked away.

LATER

Today I go to the Sumps'. It feels so bad inside me, I am scared and mad and helpless all at once. I am going away from everything I know.

Grandad Moore ran the Blue Spruce for forty years until he died three years ago when I was eleven. I still miss him. After school I'd come to the tavern, where they'd be setting up for the dinner hour. My first job was placing the spoons and forks while Grandad polished the glasses. Mama was usually writing out the menu. It changed every day. We were known for our roasts and our fish stew, and she was up and at the Reading Market every morning before sunrise.

Grandad never trusted my father, and he lived long enough to know he was right, I suppose.

"I don't trust that foreigner," he said, even though my father had lived in America most of his life. He came over from France with his parents, and he still spoke with an accent. I never knew my grandparents — they died before I was born. My father has been looking after himself since he was sixteen.

Before he married Mama he went door-to-door selling pots and pans — like a tinker, Grandad said. Looking for an easy life, he said, and Mama would snort and say, "So he came to a tavern? Didn't know I was leading the high life, old man."

My earliest memory is of my father, standing by the front door, welcoming people. Tall and black-haired like me. His name is Jacques Bonner — *Zhack Bon-ay*, it's pronounced in French, but everyone calls him Jock.

My name in French is so pretty, *Meen-ette Bon-ay*, but in American I'm just plain old Minnie Bonner.

What bothered Grandad is that the tavern wasn't good enough for my father. He was always wanting to try new dishes, to go for a fancier clientele. He had dreams, it seems to me, and what's wrong with that? But Grandad never liked how he got to act like the host. He moved around the dining room, seating people, slapping backs, raising a glass, and not hardly wiping a table or polishing a candlestick.

After Grandad died, Papa suggested that Mama take the back dining room and turn it into a room for private dinners. He convinced her that all the best restaurants did that. He started to teach the cook how to make French sauces. That's when Mr. Sump started arriving with his friends from the banks and fancy houses around Rittenhouse Square.

Papa has always been restless. The first time he disappeared for three days Mama called the police. The second time she didn't. And then it just became part of our lives, how he'd not be there one morning when I got up, and I learned not to ask. Mama made up stories for a while and then she stopped. Jock had gone for a long walk, people joked. And the men would laugh a bit, and the women would feel sorry for us, I guess, but nobody said a mean word to our faces because everybody liked Papa too much.

Here is a funny thing I just realized, diary — when I said at the beginning that my family talked about things, I never realized that we can talk and talk and talk, and yet not say one word about the most important thing.

When he'd come in the door at last, after a week or two, Mama wouldn't say a word, just put his plate and cup down on the table. And sometimes I was relieved and sometimes I was mad, and I guess I was both at the same time. He'd pick up his cup and wink at me. And I couldn't help smiling at him, because he was my papa and he made me happy. In a few hours or a few days Mama would be smiling, too. He would be calling her *"ma belle"* and bringing her onto his knee. He says her name like this: *ah-zhel*, and it sounds as soft as feathers. Much better than Hazel, isn't it? Mama has big hazel (*ah-zhel!*) eyes with long black eyelashes, but she's not named for her pretty eyes, because Grandad said they were blue like mine when she was born. She has long auburn hair to her waist and is the loveliest woman in the world except for right now when I am not speaking to her.

17

APRIL 3, 1906

Well, here I am, a maid. How do you like that, diary? I don't.

Yesterday I walked from the tavern to their house near Rittenhouse Square. It's the right district for society folk, but it's not the right house. Even I can see that. Society in Philadelphia is all about not showing off, you see. It's about how long your family has been in America, who your great-grandfather was, did he own land, was he prosperous. I know who my great-grandfather was — he started the tavern — but we are just trade folk. That makes us one step up from riffraff, I'm guessing, in this part of town.

The Sumps are rich, but that's not enough in Philadelphia. Mr. Sump made his money in real estate and invested in railroads out West. No one in Philadelphia knows his family. He says he's from Chicago. He arrived with money and made more money, buying up land north and west of the city. Mrs. Sump refers grandly to her "family in Cincinnati," but her father was a tailor. The Sumps have their noses pressed up to the fine windows of the elegant houses of Philadelphia society. They will never let them in.

Mrs. Sump thinks we don't know she's been snubbed by real society here. Maybe she doesn't realize that *all* of Philadelphia knows. It's a city of taverns and coffeehouses and gossip. Mama used to say that's how the Constitution was written, just men talking and arguing in Philadelphia taverns, and then writing it down.

You can see it, how badly Mrs. Sump wants to be noticed. The brass knocker is brighter than on anyone else's door, the blue is the wrong color, the black trim too shiny. The house is like a bully with his chest stuck out saying, *Look at me.*

I am wearing a maid's uniform. In a paper bag I have another and two aprons. I went last week to a seamstress and the money will come from my wages, nine dollars a week, except I'll only get two dollars in my pocket. The rest goes to Mama.

I have a gray dress for mornings, black for nighttime, with a long white apron and cap. I am too young to be a lady's maid but I'm tall and so people will think I'm older, I guess. And now I'll have a week's training in Mrs. Sump's house. I have no idea what I'll be doing. Polishing things. Fetching tea. Helping Miss Lily Sump dress and doing her hair. Tending to the fires and making beds.

I'd rather wash the greasiest pots in the tavern. I'd rather clean the fish.

My mother told me not to knock at the front door whatever I do. To go around to the side. The cook made me wait. The floors were full of wooden crates and spilled straw and the servants were rushing about with the packing of tureens and saucers, preparing for the great move.

I was sent up to the "morning room." Rich swells have a room they only use in the mornings! Mrs. Sump was at a desk, wearing a lilac silk gown trimmed in green ribbons. The lacework on her sleeves draped over her knuckles. She looked like a petit four melting in August heat. She gave me a ticking glance, up and down, *tick tick tick*, not bothering to hide that she was staring. I made a plan to imitate her later for my best friend, Sadie

Millman, but then I remembered that I wasn't going home.

"You're to go 'round with Bridget," she said. "She'll show you your duties. You'll come out with Lily and I on the train."

Lily and me, I thought, but I suppose it's not good to correct your employer.

"Yes, ma'am."

"Pity you don't have an accent," she said. "You *do* speak French, though?"

"Yes, ma'am, a bit," I said. I only know a little, what my father taught me. He's always spoken to me in French and tried to teach me, but it's mostly kitchen French, the names of dishes and sauces, meats and vegetables.

"Your name, Minette, your full name, that's what we'll call you. Not Minnie, you're not a tavern waitress. And don't think this will be easy— you'll work." She lifted a finger. "I don't stand for servants taking advantage."

"I'm used to working, ma'am."

"*Madame.* That's what you'll call me. And when you speak to Lily I want you to use easy French

21

phrases, you know, that she can use in conversation." I wasn't about to tell Mrs. Sump that Lily will wind up knowing the words for "boiled potatoes" or "braised with onions" instead of "if you please" and "how very kind."

She lifted her chin for a big sniff, like she was sucking down celestial air. "They have Chinese for servants out there, I hear, godless little men wearing slippers! I'll teach them a thing or two about what real society is."

I was lucky I grew up in a tavern. You learn to keep your face straight while people do or say the stupidest things. So I didn't laugh. I can't pretend to know what real society is like, but I bet Mrs. Sump doesn't know any better than I do. Look at her, she doesn't even sit like a lady, not quite. Her feet just planted on the floor, long and wide as barrel staves. You can tell by the way she picks up her cup and puts it down again. You can tell by the way she gestures. She is not grand at all, she is doing it like a play, like a charade.

"Lily will have a proper French maid," she said with satisfaction.

And then suddenly I see why I'm there, and why she made this deal with Mama. She expects to go out West to a fine city that's new, to people who won't ask who her father was. Money is all she needs. And she thinks she'll be the grand lady from Philadelphia showing them how it's done.

With a French maid. That's me.

It would be fun to laugh at her, but I guess the joke is on me.

APRIL 4, 1906

There's a butler to answer the door and a house-keeper to keep things running and a cook. There's a parlormaid — Bridget — who also waits on Mrs. Sump. Mrs. Sump speaks of how there will be a "full staff" in San Francisco, because of the larger house. Mr. Sump has already hired them out there, she says. Mrs. Sump said right in front of Bridget to her daughter, Lily, that all servants were lazy and Mr. Sump was too soft, so she might have to hire new staff herself all over again, once they settle in.

"Well, I feel sorry for 'em," Bridget said as we

all had our tea in the kitchen. "She's as tough as old boiled boots."

"Hush now, Bridget, you with your talk," the housekeeper, Mrs. Greenlee, said, but you could tell she agreed.

Bridget plopped a scone on my plate. "And I hear they murder twenty people a day out where you're going. I've got me a new position in a better house out in the country."

I don't know anything about San Francisco except what I've heard about the Barbary Coast, how it's a place of murder and gambling, but I suppose the fortunes out there are newer and shinier so things aren't the same. No matter what, I can't imagine it will be easy for Olive Sump. Who is now calling herself Olivia. I saw her practice writing it on a piece of paper.

In the meantime I lay out Lily's clothes and help to pack her trunks with Bridget and start the fires and bring the tea, and learn the right way to do things, like you can't hand your mistress a letter with your own hand, you have to put it on a tray. Just in case your skin touches hers.

LATER

Something funny happened this afternoon. Mrs. Sump canceled her shopping trip, saying she had too much to do. That meant she stood hovering over me as I counted all her gloves and set aside the ones she wants for the trip, and the others she will pack to be sent ahead, and then did the same with her shawls, boots, and coats.

She's afraid the servants will steal from her while they are packing all her things. She is afraid that the dressmaker will not finish her evening cape on time. She is afraid that the portrait artist will not properly crate the painting she posed for and it will be damaged on the way to San Francisco, and she wants to hang it in the study. And the rest of us in the house have to hear all of this, over and over and over again.

"And remember, Lily, all those afternoons we had to pose?" she said. "Will it be all for naught? You can't trust anybody, you know. Nobody knows the right way to do things. Fold that again, Minette, or it will get creased."

We heard the knocker and the butler was busy

downstairs counting the silver because Mrs. Sump would be on him next and he couldn't leave it. So he said I could answer the door and be quick about it.

A young man in a good suit handed me his card, thick white paper, ANDREW JEWELL, and I put it on the little silver tray and took it in to Mrs. Sump. She turned three kinds of red and said right out loud to Lily, "The cheek! Your father can do business with whoever he likes, but I'm not bound to receive him!" and then told me to tell the man — not the "gentleman," but the man, so that lets me see he's not society no matter how he's dressed — that she is not at home. And Lily rose and stood by the window as though to distance herself from all this, and Mrs. Sump snapped at her that young ladies should not be seen from the street.

I went back and told him that the Sumps were not at home, and I could tell that he knew it wasn't true — is being a maid all about lying as well as not talking at all? — and for a moment I saw something hard and angry in his eyes. Then he tipped his hat at me and I could see his blond hair and light amber eyes. He smiled, and I suddenly saw that he was handsome.

Didn't he know I noticed it, too! He smiled at me as though we had a secret.

Then he asked how my father was. And when I looked surprised he said, "I've seen you at the Blue Spruce."

I'd never noticed him. I suppose he was just one in a pack of young gentlemen of business coming in.

"Tell him I sent my regards," he said. He picked the card off the tray and handed it to me. "We might have some things in common."

I wanted to say, *Well, I don't see how.* Or, *He's gone off for good, so keep your fancy card.* I didn't appreciate his familiarity. But I just put it in my apron pocket.

He took a step back and looked at the house and then had the nerve to wink at me before he walked away.

Well, that was a peculiar thing.

In the meantime I am running all 'round this

house with lists of things to do, trying to please Lily with her remote airs and her round blank face. She is almost pretty when she smiles, but I've only seen that once when I brought her letters to her and she thanked me. Usually she seems to be just daydreaming her way through her life, which I guess you can do when you're rich.

So I find that I'm not really training to be a lady's maid, I'm just lifting and sorting and packing. I don't think I'm here for training at all. I think I'm here to be an extra pair of hands. Bridget and I pack trunk after trunk with clothes that will be sent ahead, and then we have to unpack them when Mrs. Sump decides she must have this gown or that petticoat with her for the journey and for her first week there. Last night she kept Bridget up until one in the morning. I just watch it all and think, *This is now my life, watching a mean rich lady get everything she wants when I've lost everything.*

APRIL 5, 1906

Bridget just up and quit! She left two days early for her new job, and wasn't Mrs. Sump in a fit. But

Bridget was smart, because she's going to work at the country estate of Mrs. Thomas Whitford out in Merion, and she is one of the big society ladies, so Mrs. Sump is too afraid to cross her. Ha!

"I don't know why I'm so plagued with trouble," Mrs. Sump said. "Servants just take advantage."

LATER THAT NIGHT

I am so tired. I am writing this by candlelight. Bridget is gone and so I'm alone in the little maid's room up in the attic. It's funny to see how grand houses use all their space downstairs for rooms too big for the family and yet the servants above are stuffed into these tiny bare spaces. When you look at a big house from the outside, you never expect there would be rooms crammed in so small at the top.

Oh, there is so much left to do.

I have never imagined that one person would need so many tea gowns, and ball gowns, and skirts and bodices and petticoats of taffeta and silk and organdy, and gloves, and shawls, and fans, and corsets, and hats.

But it is easy to wait on Lily Sump. She doesn't talk.

Tonight when she unclasped her bracelet (she's not used to having a lady's maid, I'm supposed to do that, Bridget told me) I said, "May I help you with that, miss?" and she shook her head. She was standing by the window, and, diary, I think she said this:

"No one can help me."

So I stood still, and waited, because I didn't know what to do.

But then she just smiled and said, "I can manage, Minette," and I think maybe I did not hear what I thought I heard.

APRIL 8, 1906

I was allowed to come home to say good-bye today. Mama had already moved to the rooming house near the river. Her room was small and crammed with just a bed and a table. Mildew stained the walls. I could hear the person in the next room coughing.

"Did you say good-bye to Sadie?" Mama asked me.

I had been thinking I would stop by and say a last good-bye to my best friend. But in the end I couldn't. I would write to her, I decided. I couldn't stand to see pity in her eyes, her and her mother. Everybody feeling sorry for us—that was almost worse than anything that happened.

I gave Mama the card from Andrew Jewell and she looked at it like she'd just discovered a rat on the table.

"Where did you see him?" she asked, and I told her he came to call on the Sumps but Mrs. Sump wouldn't let him in.

"I'm not surprised at that," she said.

I asked her why, but she wouldn't say. She looked so small and tired, sitting in that awful room.

"How long?" I asked. "How long do I have to be in that house, working off the debt?" And I finally was able to say how I felt. "It's awful, Ma. I hate it."

She didn't want to hear that. I saw it in her face. She wanted me to be like a girl in a book, all

31

brave and stalwart and cheerful. Instead of miserable and afraid and angry.

Two years isn't so very long, she said. I've done some figuring, and I'll be able to put enough by in two years to get a proper place for us to live. It will be gone in a blink of an eye.

I made an exaggerated blink. "Still here," I said.

And this was when the fight began.

Mama said she still deserved my respect.

Why, I said. Why wasn't money set by for hard times? That's what Grandad always did. How did they manage to lose every cent we had?

All the money went back into the tavern, she said. It was fine because we had a place that was ours.

So I said, if I'm old enough to be sent away to help out, I'm old enough to know.

Here is something I learned, diary: Sometimes it is better not to know, I think.

Here is what she said, the words spilling out so fast:

"Your father is the reason we are here like this, left with nothing. He lost it, he lost everything. He was so proud to be invited into that back room, with the rich men gambling. Yes, Min, they were playing cards. And when this man" — and she shook the card at me — "this Andrew Jewell won all that money, he demanded it all right away. He made threats against your father. He said he knew people in the police department who would shut down the tavern. He wouldn't wait for his money, and why should he, really, since he won it? So Mr. Sump took pity on your father and gave him a loan to cover the debt. He said not to worry about paying it back, he wouldn't charge interest, but to use the tavern as collateral. And then suddenly he says because of this move to San Francisco his partners insisted on him collecting. So your father had to give up the tavern."

"But how could he have left?" I asked. "Without even saying good-bye to me?" Diary, I tried not to sound like a little girl when I asked that. Even though I felt like one. "Why did he leave for good? Why didn't he stay and help?"

That's when she said he didn't leave, she threw him out. She said to go away and never come back.

"So there's no forgiveness?" I asked her.

"Not for this," she said. "I was a sap. A silly fool with my head in the clouds. Your father is a gambler, Min. That's why he goes away and comes back. He gambles and loses and can't face me. So yes, all our money was tied up in the tavern. We could never get ahead.

"It's up to us now, Min," she said. "We will start over from scratch. We can do it. I wish I could do it with you beside me, but I can't." She said she couldn't bear to bring me here, that I would be living in a fine house, that Mrs. Sump had promised to look after me.

"I could get a job," I said. "I could work in a factory. I could say I was sixteen or seventeen, people would believe it. I always get taken for older than I am."

No, she said. Not that life. That would be worse.

"This is worse!" I screamed.

And I said I hated her for it.

And I ran out the door.

34

LATER
MIDNIGHT

I am packed and ready to leave tomorrow. My life hadn't seemed quite so small before. Now it is something you could hold in your fist. Just a few things in a suitcase.

Look, diary, how the paper is all splotched and sodden. I didn't think there were so many tears in the world.

APRIL 10, 1906

What a time getting on the train! She fussed and fussed, getting settled with all her parcels and boxes, and then when she saw my little suitcase she complained about my taking up too much room!

And Lily, what a creature, doesn't say much just follows behind her ma's big behind.

I haven't had a minute to myself, not even to cry.

APRIL 11, 1906

We changed trains in Chicago and now we're going all the way through to California. Mrs. Sump and Lily are in the fancy Pullman car where they swivel the seats at night and make lovely private beds for you, but I have to sleep sitting up. I don't mind. I get to have a whole seven hours without her voice in my ear. I do not think she stopped talking for one minute altogether yesterday.

I sit and lean my head against the window and wait for the towns, when the conductor swings his lantern in the dark as we pass, and the people asleep in their houses make us a part of their dreams.

APRIL 12, 1906

The days are full of her complaints, too hot, no too cold, needs tea, find her pillow, mend her gloves. Not allowed to rest until she's sleeping and then I fall asleep like a rock fell on my head.

And the train wheels on the track are saying this: *You're alone you're alone you're alone.*

LATER

She keeps a green case with her always, right by her feet. I am guessing it holds her jewelry because even I can't pick it up and she makes me carry everything.

This morning she shouted at me in front of the whole car and called me "ignorant girl" when her tea wasn't hot enough.

I am not so ignorant. I know this much: She is a terrible old thing.

LATER

I am finally able to write. We have our routines now. In the afternoons she falls asleep after lunch.

Mrs. Sump has made a list of all the eligible bachelors in San Francisco. Lily is sixteen so she has two years, Mrs. Sump said, before the bloom is off the rose. Courting by seventeen, engaged by eighteen and a half, married by twenty, she said. Lily just stared out the window.

She's been studying up, and she's got the names.

She's going to start with the wife of Mr. Sump's lawyer, she told Lily — Mrs. Hugh Crandall. Not that she's *quite* the upper crust, but she is invited to the bigger events. She's a second cousin to one of the big San Francisco families, so the Crandalls, according to Mrs. Sump, have managed to climb their way to the lower rungs of society, despite being "in trade."

"That will be my entrée," she said. "One always needs an entrée at first."

And she plants her feet on her green case and gossips about people she doesn't know, about who would be "suitable" or not. She talks about the great San Francisco families like she knows them. I've become her secretary, for I have to copy down who she expects to call on within the first six months. De Young and the Spreckels and Hopkins and Flood and Crocker and Tevis and Haggin and Kohl. And sometimes she mentions a young man's name, and she frowns and considers.

"Maybe he'll do," she says.

Lily stares out the window.

APRIL 13, 1906

Lily's not a bad sort, although I have to say, she does not seem to possess a sense of humor. Perhaps because she seems sad.

You can tell that she is ashamed a bit of her mother, when Mrs. Sump is rude to the porter. She calls them all "George" no matter who they are. I don't think she can tell them apart.

Maybe it's being on a train—you get to see the bad up close, the people who complain and the people who make the best of it. You get to smell the perspiration and the bad breath so why not the bad character, too?

When Mrs. Sump falls asleep for her nap, Lily tells me she's going to get some fresh air so she walks to the back of the train to stand on the platform. She is always back by the time Mrs. Sump wakes up. No doubt she just wants to be alone. I know how she feels.

I just realized that *Sump* rhymes with *grump*. Ha!

MIDNIGHT

What a big country this is!

I'm used to the rocking now. We all are. And I'm almost used to sleeping sitting up. I try to stay awake to write this. We're well past the Mississippi River now. The sky is the biggest thing I've ever seen. Stars tossed across it. Prairie out the window, miles of it. And every once in a while, the stars fall and gather in a tiny twinkling heap, and that's a town.

APRIL 14, 1906

We'll be going over the mountains today. I have to say I'm looking forward to that. I can't help it. Everyone is excited to see California.

Is this why Papa left us all the time? Just to go somewhere else? Just to see something new, just to breathe new air? I'm wondering about that. Because there is something exhilarating about it.

California is a place to start over. Maybe I'll never go home.

I struck up a conversation with a man traveling with his family. I know he was a stranger, and you're not supposed to speak to strangers, but boundaries tend to fall away on a train. He was telling his son about San Francisco and I couldn't help but listen. I really don't know much about it, and Bridget's warnings didn't help.

But he told me that it's a grand city. With a great big park that sweeps out to the ocean, and a bustling downtown and a busy port with ships sailing to Japan and all through the Pacific. He said that it is a city of hills and valleys, and almost everyplace you walk there is a view. The hills are so steep they have to use streetcars that are pulled up on cables. There are nickelodeons and vaudeville theatres and grand hotels and a dish called a Hangtown fry, which is scrambled eggs and oysters, and he said it was the best dish he ever ate. There are two opera houses in San Francisco! Enrico Caruso, the most famous opera singer in the world, is scheduled to perform the very night we arrive. I have heard Mr. Caruso singing from the phonograph. I can't imagine hearing that glorious voice in person.

Lily said a funny thing today. I was washing

out her mother's stockings in the sink. The water is so cold. My hands were red and I rubbed them on the thin towel, then rolled the stockings in it to dry them. And Lily said this:

"Doesn't it make you think, traveling by train?"

I looked over at her. She was watching the landscape blur outside the window, flat and dry.

"You pass so many towns. And you can't help but think there are so many ways to live. You can't help seeing what a different life could be like."

Then she looked at me. "You could do that. You could just get off at a stop and start over."

"I hardly think so, miss," I said, all proper. I just kept wringing out the stockings.

"You don't know what it's like to feel trapped."

I kept my head down, because I couldn't believe she was saying that to me. To *me*.

I don't know if rich folk can really see anyone but themselves, I truly don't.

"All she wants to do is marry me off to someone richer than we are," Lily said.

I got the nerve to look up then, and I think she was crying.

Before I could muster up a word she turned and went down the aisle toward the back of the train. After a minute or two I followed her, my conscience pricking me because I hadn't comforted her, even with a word or two. Maybe I could ask if she'd care for tea. So I went to the back of the train and there she was, standing outside on the platform, her back to me. I started forward but I saw then that someone else was out there, a slender man in a derby hat, and I could tell they were conversing, so I turned right around.

Let her have her pleasures, the fresh air, the casual remarks of a stranger to pass the time. She was right, I suppose. Soon enough she'd be back in her mother's web.

Maybe Lily is as alone as I am.

APRIL 15, 1906
SUNDAY
6 A.M.

The snoring of the fat man across the aisle woke me up, but I don't mind. Sunrise is pink and orange and you can still see the pale half moon.

I am homesick.

Sundays the tavern was closed. It was the only day my mother slept past five A.M. It was the day we had the tavern kitchen to ourselves. My father cooked breakfast and dinner, and taught me how to make sauces and stews.

Early in the morning my father used to wake me up and we'd tiptoe down the back staircase into the big kitchen.

Breakfast together. Just us.

He made eggs and grilled toast and bacon and put the egg on top of the bread with the bacon, too. It was the best breakfast in the world. Sometimes he would tell me about growing up in Lille, France, and sometimes he would tell me about his parents. His father was a chef in a fancy hotel in New York but lost his job. Then his parents were killed in a streetcar accident and he took off so that they wouldn't send him to an orphanage.

I asked him how he got along, and he would just smile and say that there are always ways to make money for young boys who don't mind a bit of trouble. He learned how to play cards, too.

Which is what got *us* into trouble, I guess.

The last time we had our Sunday breakfast was a few days before he left. I knew that things were not right between my parents. I woke myself up on Sunday morning and found him on the back stoop, drinking the strong black coffee he liked. He had forgotten to wake me up, I accused him, and I remembered how he looked up, startled, and I saw the lines around his blue eyes and that his skin sagged a little on his cheeks.

We went into the kitchen and this time I made breakfast because he looked so tired. I cracked eggs and cut butter into flour and made biscuits and bacon and served him.

We ate without talking. When we were done he thanked me and said I was so grown up now and could take care of myself, couldn't I. And I boasted that I could.

Why did I say that, diary? Why didn't I say, *I'm not grown up, Papa, I still need you*? Was I giving him permission to leave me?

I asked him why he left us all the time and he said my mother had the most honest eyes in the world and sometimes it was hard to meet them. So he goes away, but then his heart is with my mother and with me and he cannot live without his heart.

Then he kissed me and held me against his chest. He called me his treasure, and then *ma poulette*. Which means "little hen," diary. I said a hen is hardly a treasure and he said, "It is if you need eggs."

That's the last time we laughed together. It seemed to hurt him to laugh.

A few days later he was gone.

APRIL 17, 1906

This was my first day in San Francisco, and I'm going to start from the beginning and remember everything I saw and every word I heard. I'll have to write this in pieces, I know, because there is still so much work to be done.

Oh, the bustle of Oakland as we got off the train and onto the ferry! The crush of the people and the porters yelling and Mrs. Sump trying to push ahead.

But once we were on the ferry I got to stand

against the rail and watch the city come closer and closer. It is a city of hills that spill down to the bay, and houses hugging those hills, clinging for dear life. I would like to live in a house like that, open to sea and sky.

It was a gray day, with a fine drizzle out on the water. A layer of fog lay on the water to the west. Everything was gray and silver and blue.

When we docked, there was no Mr. Sump. Mrs. Sump was furious.

Then a gleaming new Oldsmobile pulled up, and it was for us! It was so exciting! The driver found us and it turned out it was the lawyer Mr. Crandall's car. Mr. Sump had sent it for us.

"He would have come himself, ma'am, but he figured you'd need the room for your bags and boxes and your maid," the driver said, tipping his cap.

Mrs. Sump inhaled sharply, as if she'd smelled something awful instead of heard it. But she cheered up when she saw lots of folks looking enviously at the machine.

The rest of our things would come by cart.

I ran back and forth directing the porter because Mrs. Sump couldn't decide which she had to have in the car and which could go by cart, and all was confusion, especially when we lost Lily for about ten minutes. But we were finally settled. I'd never ridden in an automobile before. I got in the front next to the driver, and Lily and Mrs. Sump got in back with some of our boxes and bags and cases.

It was thrilling, diary. I can't wait to write Mama about it, as soon as I'm not angry at her anymore. We couldn't go very fast because we were on a street with streetcars and traffic — Market Street, the driver said.

I'm a city girl and not afraid of traffic or bustle, but this city is wild and noisy, with the hooves of the horses clanging on the streetcar rails and people dashing across the street just missing being trampled or knocked into next week. So many telegraph and telephone wires strung overhead, so many groups of men standing and talking as though the news was depending on what they thought of it. The driver pointed to a skyscraper known as the Call Building—eighteen stories, he said! All of us twisted and craned our necks to see the elegant Palace Hotel and to watch ladies sweeping by in extravaganzas of hats, out for a day of shopping and luncheon.

Then we turned a corner—going so fast, I was afraid I'd tumble out—and the driver pointed out a pretty square—Union Square, he said, and then past the St. Francis Hotel and, oh dear, we went straight up a hill so steep I thought we'd fall backward! I was breathless with it.

When we got to the top, the bay reappeared again, grayish blue, and beyond it were hills, round and huddled together like the backs of sleeping bears. Marin County, the driver said, with Sausalito nestled at the bottom, right on the bay.

"Is this Nob Hill?" Mrs. Sump asked, leaning forward.

"Yes, ma'am. That's the old Mark Hopkins mansion there—now it's an art league. And that big white building is the new Fairmont Hotel, opening soon. Here is the Stanford house, the Huntington house, the Floods . . ." and with every millionaire's name you could see the satisfaction growing on Mrs. Sump's face.

We crested the hill and started down the other side, and that's when she got to fidgeting. The driver pulled up in front of a big house with bay windows and turrets and four white columns in front. There was a stack of slate in the yard. An empty barrel lay on its side, and a shovel leaned against it as though it had been tossed aside and just left there in the middle of a job.

"This," Mrs. Sump said, in her iciest voice, "cannot possibly be it."

And of course the driver said yes ma'am and Mrs. Sump's nostrils flared like a horse's, and that look came on her face like she'd like to kick you if she was allowed.

"Is this still Nob Hill?" she said.

"Yes, ma'am, milady," the driver said. He sounded so nervous, like he didn't know what was wrong but knew it would get blamed on him. I know that feeling from waiting on Mrs. Sump. "Just a bit on the down slope, is all."

Mrs. Sump turned pale. "The *down* slope?"

And then the door opened and out came Mr. Sump, his matchstick legs sticking out from under his big belly, and his smile wide and uneasy.

"My dear!" he said.

He came toward the car with his arms out and I thought he was going to help her down but he reached toward her feet instead, and came back with the green case. So the driver had to help her out, and she didn't like that one bit.

Nothing like starting out on the wrong foot.

She complained about him not being there, and he told her there's an explanation, but she should get settled first and see the house, and he kissed Lily's forehead and smiled at her fondly and ignored me. I curtsied but he didn't see.

The driver took all the cases and things inside and then drove off, no doubt glad to get away.

They went in front of me into the house and I couldn't believe Mrs. Sump didn't stop for a minute just to look at how pretty it was, so different from the dull brick of their town house back in Philadelphia.

The view was of downtown on one side and the

bay on the other . . . your thoughts fly away just looking at it. I had to hurry to catch up with them.

I walked into the house and just stopped for a moment. I tried not to gawk, but it was hard. The hall was high ceilinged and was more like a gallery, for it ran the length of the house, all polished wood, floor and ceiling. Through an archway I glimpsed a parlor magnificent with gilt and marble and paintings and tapestries. There was a big marble mantel over the fireplace and a carved wood ceiling. I walked a little farther to see the grand curving stairway with the stone banister.

There was so much carving and gilt and draperies and tapestries and marble and stone that I felt overstuffed, like I'd eaten a supper of lobster and duck and roast beef and finished it all off with cream puffs.

They stood right in the grand entrance, and Mrs. Sump asked where the butler was. That's when Mr. Sump told the story.

Jiminy, you never heard such an explosion with the two of them shouting over each other. I didn't even have to eavesdrop, big as the house is, I just had to stand still in the hallway and I heard it all.

First of all, all the servants Mr. Sump had hired have been hired away! He has a business rival, it seems, who wanted to get back at him for something. ("Something trifling," Mr. Sump said, "after all, this is business, what is the man thinking?") So he blackballed him from the Pacific Union Club, whatever that is, and then hired away all the servants just this morning, doubling their salaries. So they just walked out! It's almost enough to make you laugh, these two rich men squabbling like bullies in a playground. But it means I'm the only one here to fetch and carry. So I'm not laughing.

I heard Mr. Sump tell Mrs. Sump that San Francisco has been built on bribes and he doesn't mind paying his way but he doesn't believe in being taken advantage of.

But she wasn't listening, so she took on a full head of steam like a locomotive charging up the Sierra Nevada, so angry about the lack of servants and the fact that the house isn't on the crown of the hill. No matter that there wasn't a parcel to buy, he should have made it happen. Offer a person money for his house and then knock it down and build something better! Isn't that how he made his fortune?

And he said that they have a magnificent home on Nob Hill and nothing he does ever satisfies her. I saw Lily drifting back and finding a doorway to disappear into. But I was stuck. If I went forward they'd see me, and my back was to the front door so I couldn't leave.

Mrs. Sump sat down with a crash on a spindly piece of furniture and said how can she be satisfied when she doesn't even have a cook or a housekeeper, and don't he be thinking he can hire those godless Chinese.

And he said many of the houses use the Chinese and they make good workers. And I'd have to agree with him because didn't they build the railroad?

But Mrs. Sump just started wailing again and saying they'll never get Lily properly married if they can't be society folk, because what hope does she have, with that plain face? Which I think Lily might have heard because I heard a door slam.

Mr. Sump stomped off, saying he'd had enough

of female hysteria and his life had been a lot more serene living in a hotel.

So Mrs. Sump heard this and said, yes, that's what she'll do, go to a hotel, and not the residence hotel he's been staying at, but the Palace. Because the house isn't even done!

And Mr. Sump roared that they'll do it over his dead body because he built this house for his family and by God they're going to live in it.

And then she wondered if the house is too small.

Small! It's bigger than their house in Philadelphia, and grander, too. Gilt mirrors and marble tables and woodwork curling along and back onto itself in every which way, and chandeliers and a staircase with a landing big enough for a sofa. I think she was just finding fault to punish him.

Mr. Sump promised that tomorrow the agency will send new servants to interview for the jobs, and certainly there will be a cook by nightfall. In the meantime they can make do.

Mrs. Sump doesn't care to make do.

The cart arrived then, so I ran out to supervise the unloading of the rest of the trunks. They piled everything in the front hall and I directed them to carry the trunks up to the bedrooms, running up and down to say where to put things — and having to guess where she would want them. I remembered to count everything and made sure everything was there.

I forgot to look for my own suitcase. By the time I realized it was missing, the cart was gone.

Two uniforms, three aprons, plus my own day-off dress and boots. All my clothes, so carefully mended and packed. Slippers and a wrapper and my books! Paper to write letters. Thank goodness I had my diary in my pocket.

But I'll have to tell Mrs. Sump, and I don't have one particle of faith that it won't get blamed on me.

LATER

I haven't found the suitcase or told Mrs. Sump yet. There is so much to do! I had to leave off writing to start unpacking the trunks. Tonight Mr.

Sump has bought tickets to Enrico Caruso in *Carmen*. They're to dine out at the Palace Hotel beforehand and go to Delmonico's after, which is just about the fanciest restaurant in town. Well, didn't that set Mrs. Sump to rights. She is now proclaiming what a fine and generous man he is.

Such a flurry now, for all of San Francisco society will be there and Mrs. Sump must wear her gold gown and her pearls.

Oh, diary, you should see her bedroom. A thick Turkey rug on the floor and you never saw such an enormous mirror. Her bed is the size of three or four of my bed at home. There are four posts sticking up that make a cage above the bed. There are supposed to be draperies that hang over it, but they haven't arrived yet. (You can imagine how she felt about *that*.) Porcelain vases almost as tall as I am and full of peacock feathers. She is unhappy because the marble mantel ordered from Italy has not been installed. It's propped against the wall. Chinese vases, Turkey carpet, Italian mantel, French drapes—if you stood in the middle of the room and twirled, you'd get yourself a walloping trip 'round the world.

If I had this room, I would leave it almost bare and maybe just have a few things, white and blue and gray. Then I'd have a little armchair right by the window so I could just look out the window at the view. A breeze has sprung up and pushed the fog away. I have never seen anything like this blue bay and soft hills.

I wouldn't like to live in a mansion. But I would like a little house with a view of all that blue.

My own room is in the attic. It is small and spare, but I didn't expect any better. There're two more beds in it, so I'll have to share. There is a view of the chimneys.

There was another argument when Lily said she had a headache and would not take tea with them. Mrs. Sump said she couldn't stay in her room and sulk, this was their home now. Mr. Sump told Mrs. Sump to let the poor child alone and bade me to bring her a cold cloth for her forehead and her tea on a tray. So that's what I did.

Here's what happened just now. I need to set it down just as I heard it so I can study it later. I don't know what to think.

I brought the tea tray into the study. Mr. Sump had the green case on the desk and was unlocking it. He waited, his hands on the lid, until I'd left the room.

So I waited outside in the hall to listen. Just for a moment, I decided. I was dying to know what was in the case.

It isn't jewelry. It's money. Cash money.

"I was terrified the whole journey," Mrs. Sump said. "I could have been murdered in cold blood."

"But you weren't."

"I don't understand why I couldn't wire the money."

I heard sounds of footsteps and then something opening. Something clanged.

"Sometimes in business, my dear, it is better not to have a record of things."

"I did as you asked, Chester." I heard the clatter of a teacup. "I don't have to understand it, but I do follow your orders. And tell me this: Why does that Jewell character have the cheek to call on us? What did he do for you?"

"Never mind. He did his job and he's been paid handsomely for it," Mr. Sump said. "He had certain skills I required. We won't see him again."

Now I *needed* to hear this. Curiosity pushed me down the hall and next door to the reception room. There are double doors in the study that lead to the reception room, I guess so they can be thrown open if the Sumps throw a big party. I stole inside and while Mrs. Sump was talking I cracked open those doors. I could see right to the desk where Mr. Sump sat.

My heart was a hammer. *Bang!Bang!Bang!*

He was writing something in a book.

Mrs. Sump asked if he was listening to her.

He still said nothing.

"What are you *doing*?" she asked, her voice rising.

"The secret to success in business," he said, blowing on the ink and then snapping the book closed, "is two sets of books."

"I don't understand you."

"That's all right, my dear. You don't have to."

He rose and went to the fireplace. There was paneling along the sides, all carved images of leaves and fruit and flowers. It had been painted in gold. His back was to me and he must have pressed something, because the paneling slid up and disappeared into the wall.

Mrs. Sump looked up from the tea table. "Whatever are you doing?"

"I had them conceal the safe."

"How clever! What is the combination? I should put my jewels in it."

I was closer to Mr. Sump and I only heard him say:

"My precious flower."

Which was odd, because I never heard him call her anything nicer than "my dear," and even that he said in a businesslike way.

She asked for the combination again and he just said she never pays attention to him. He took out a large strongbox and brought it to the desk. Then he reached for his pocket watch. I couldn't see what he did — there must have been a key on the chain — because he unlocked the strongbox and then put the bundles of cash and some papers and the book inside.

"Here it is, my dear. What you brought will finance our life here for several years. It took me two years of planning to buy up that one square block. Now Philadelphia will have its department store on Spruce Street, and I will have my money, and you will have your society life. Crandall leaves tomorrow to finalize the last deal."

"I'm sure you're very clever," Mrs. Sump said. "Tea?"

Spruce. That's where the tavern is! Could that be the "last deal"? My head was spinning with it all.

Mrs. Sump sipped her tea and said she hopes his poker days are over and he said yes, but if there's an advantage to be had in business he'll seize it, no matter how. And for her to stop questioning him about business matters. Sometimes he needs men like Mr. Jewell in his employ. They are useful, and that is that.

"I thought those types were behind us," Mrs.

Sump said, and he laughed. "You're joking, Olive. San Francisco is full of them," he said. "They're running the town! It's glorious. Wide open city. And that's why we're going to just get richer."

I don't care what she said next because my head was already buzzing with all those words, and I'm still trying to sort it out.

Mr. Sump *paid* Andrew Jewell? What did Mr. Sump mean when he said *he did his job*? And *he had certain skills*. . . . And his poker days are behind him. . . .

And the look on Andrew Jewell's face when he was turned away at the door.

It is too much for my head to sort out. But I will.

I want to see what is in that book.

I'm in the kitchen, which is three times the size of our old apartment, with rooms running off it for the housekeeper and the butler, and there's a butler's pantry to lay out plates and things that leads to the dining room and there's a food pantry, too, that's already been stocked, so that's good. I'll have to make some kind of breakfast tomorrow so I need to look into the larder and figure out the stove, which isn't a problem. I am used to a big kitchen. Mrs. Sump said of course she didn't expect me to act as cook, but a breakfast of eggs and ham and toast and corned beef and porridge would be acceptable.

I had my own tea sitting at the big long servant's table, just me and cheese and bread and tea. It is lovely how food in your belly can make you feel better about almost anything. My head is clearer now to think.

Except what do I know of business deals?

I do know about ledgers. Mama kept a ledger for the tavern and showed me how it worked, how you write amounts in columns, what money you take in and what money you pay out. We only had one ledger, however.

The bell will ring in a moment summoning me to get the tea things in either Lily's room or the study.

When I unpacked Lily's trunk I took a nightgown so I'd have something for tonight. She has six. I took the one with the tear at the hem, so I could say that I took it for mending if I get caught. One handkerchief, because she has at least ten, her initials embroidered on them, and not by her, I'll tell you, because the stitches are so neat. I've seen her embroidery.

I don't have a day off until next week. Tomorrow I'll need a uniform. I'll have to tell Mrs. Sump that I need clothes, but I'm not looking forward to that conversation. She'll have to advance me money. She will certainly blame me — she could fire me, with the temper she's in. As much as I don't want to be here, I want even less to land back home in disgrace, fired on my first real day.

And now I have to find out what Mr. Sump knows and I do not about the sale of the tavern.

We lost the tavern.

Papa gambled it away.

His fault.

But what if someone . . . pushed him?

Right here is where a knock came at the kitchen door, so loud it made me jump. That is the spill of the tea here that I circled. Next to it is the name JAKE, for me to remember.

I opened the door. A dark-haired boy in a cap stood outside with a carton in his arms. "Delivery," he said, as if it wasn't obvious by the greens sticking out. He followed me inside and put the carton down on the counter but didn't leave.

He said something about how he'd been walking by this house every day, and how fast it went up. That's the way of it in San Francisco, he said. The quicker the better — it was the talk of Nob Hill. Had I seen City Hall yet? Now there's a building, though they say that bribes and payoffs got it built.

I didn't answer, because the rush of words didn't leave me much room.

"Heard all the servants quit and went over to the Langley house on Clay." The boy shook his head. "Hoo boy, what a dustup. Then the workmen up and quit, too."

"You seem to know the business of this house very well," I said in my most prim voice.

"Aw, not really. It's not like I'm a snoop, if that's

what you're saying. I've been here with deliveries while the cook built up the larder. Mrs. Pyle — she was a good sort, and what a cook! Gave me a ham biscuit once. She told me what's what the very day she left, how Mr. Langley himself knocked on the back door and offered them double their salaries to leave. And they had no loyalty built up to Sump, you see. They'd only been here for two weeks, setting up the household. And in that time they saw what it would be like, working here, so they left. They didn't like your boss much."

Nor do I, but I'll keep that to myself.

"Don't worry, though, I'm sure he's not as bad as all that," he said, because I guess I looked worried.

He asked me where I was from and I told him Philadelphia and then he whistled and said he's a born and bred Californian and never been east of Oakland.

I didn't want to be seen standing there chatting with a delivery boy. But then I thought maybe I need him to help me. I do have a little bit of money Mama gave me back in Philadelphia, ten dollars, and with that I could buy a uniform I'm sure, it being so plain. I could buy a few things to tide me over. Maybe then I wouldn't have to tell Mrs. Sump I lost my suitcase. I asked him if there was a seamstress nearby.

"'Course there is, this is San Francisco, greatest city west of Chicago. Plenty of 'em. But why don't you try a department store for ready-made things? First off there's City of Paris down by Union Square. You don't know where that is, do you?"

"We passed it on the way. I haven't seen much of the city."

"All right, then." He plucked a package of carrots wrapped in brown paper out of the box and then fished a stubby pencil out of his pocket.

"You're here, see? On Sacramento Street." He drew thick lines on the paper, sketching quickly. "This here is California Street—that's where you might have seen the big mansions, Crocker and Huntington, and the new Fairmont Hotel. If you walk down that street, straight down, and then turn right on Powell, you'll be at Union Square. Or you could catch the cable car from here for a corking ride down the hill. The Powell Street line will take you right to the square, and then if you look straight across you'll see the City of Paris department store right here." He grinned. "Might be too expensive for the likes of us, but there's plenty of other stores. There's a place on Mason Street for more working folk, I can give you the address." He wrote it down on the paper.

He gave me another look and unwrapped more clean space on the paper. "Look here, it's not hard to get around once you get a few facts straight. San Francisco is all up and down, it's true, but we've got water on nearly all sides, so you can almost always figure out where you are — if you climb to the top of the nearest hill," he added, grinning.

He drew more quick lines. "Here's the ocean — that's as far west as you can get. See this rectangle? That's Golden Gate Park — runs all the way out to the Pacific. You can take the streetcar out there and wade in the ocean — jiminy, it's cold. See this sort of squarish space? The Presidio, where the Army is. It goes down to the bay. You could walk it in a morning if you wanted to. This big wide street here is Van Ness. It starts at the bay and runs right up like this. Here's City Hall, and here's Chinatown. And this here's the Barbary Coast, you don't want to venture there. On this side is Telegraph Hill and here's Russian Hill, where I live. Not too far from here." He smiled at my confused face. "You'll get it. On your days off, you can explore."

"I only have one day off."

"Me too. I work at Jennardi's as a delivery boy most days after school, and then hauling crates of whiskey down at Hotaling's on Saturdays. Say, you wouldn't have a night off tonight, would you? Because down at Mechanics' Pavilion they're having a roller-skating contest. You wouldn't be going just with me," he said quickly, "if that's what you're thinking. I'm going with my sister and brother and cousins—a big group. You'll be well chaperoned. Should be a shindig. And for once it isn't damp and chilly. Feels like the first day of spring out there."

I couldn't for the life of me imagine going

to Mrs. Sump and asking if I could go roller-skating on my first night here. I laughed, and the boy looked hurt.

"I think it's a bit early to be asking for a night off, don't you?" I pointed out to him. "I don't want to get my ears boxed on my first day."

"Well, that depends," Jake said with a genial grin. "You might consider it breaking in a new boss, letting 'em know what they're in for." He pointed to the tea tray. "And if you're the only one here, roller skates might help you with chores."

I laughed, thinking of skating on the polished, elegant floor, bringing the tea tray to the study. "That would be a sight," I said. "I don't know how to roller-skate, or ice-skate, either. I'd smash the tea set before I got across the kitchen."

"That's why you have to come with us tonight. All you need is practice."

We grinned at each other, and then I felt awkward, like he might think I was forward, or flirting with him. There's no telling what he was thinking. So I busied myself taking the things out of the carton.

He edged toward the door. "I'm sure we'll meet again. I do the deliveries, like I said. I'm Jake Jennardi, by the way. Yeah, my family owns the store. We're right down the hill on Broadway."

I knew he was waiting for me to supply my name, but I hesitated. I didn't like how familiar he was.

"Aw, that's all right. You want to wait for a proper introduction I reckon. You'll find we're a bit more informal here." I stiffened, thinking he was making fun, but he touched his fingers to his cap and whistled as he headed for the door. "Well, I can wait. Good-bye, Philadelphia."

Couldn't help smiling at that while I folded up his map and tucked it between your pages, diary.

8 P.M.

Lily refused to go to the opera. Another scene. Mrs. Sump said it was the perfect opportunity for her debut into society. Mrs. Sump doesn't care about some Italian singer, but everyone will be there and they must be, too.

But Lily said her headache was worse. I don't

72

blame her — if I had that woman yammering at me like that, my head would pound, too.

I've laid out Mrs. Sump's nightclothes and I've checked on Lily, knocking on her door and hearing her say she's fine and she's going to bed.

Mr. Sump stopped me outside in the hall, saying he wanted to make sure I could find everything and apologizing for not having other servants tonight and my having to do everything.

And of course I curtsied and said I was fine, sir.

That's when he said to me that he would appreciate my telling him if any communication arrived for Lily at any time, because he would like to examine it first, being her father. He must have seen the reluctance on my face, because he said he is the head of the house and even though I wait on Miss Sump I take orders from him.

"I've been a benefactor to your family, Minette," he said. "I was happy to be able to extend a hand of generosity to an unfortunate circumstance so that a worthy family would not slide into poverty and disgrace. It's not that I expect thanks" — and here he paused, diary, so that I could dip into a small curtsy and thank him — "but I do expect loyalty."

Was that what my father was, an unfortunate circumstance? Not a person?

"I'm prepared to be loyal to you both, sir," I said, which wasn't much of an answer and by the scowl on his face he knew it.

MIDNIGHT

I am waiting up for the Sumps to return. She could want some tea, she said, and help getting into her nightclothes. With all those buttons and clasps, I'm sure she's right. I am so tired. I have to be up at five to start the fires in the rooms.

Earlier in the evening I knocked on Lily's door to collect her tea tray and she wasn't there. When I looked out the window I saw her walking quickly down the hill toward the house. I imagine she wanted some fresh air for her headache, and who could blame her? I took the tea tray and fixed up her bed again and then laid out her nightclothes.

I will fetch and carry and sew on buttons and lay out nightgowns but I will not be a spy.

If you ask me, that girl just needs to breathe some fresh air and get away from both her parents, Mrs. Sump's yammering and Mr. Sump treating her like a doll.

Now I will tell you how long it took to get Mrs. Sump into her splendid gown! Oof! Thirty buttons down her back, twenty buttons on her gloves, the diamond headpiece placed just so, the pearls clasped around her throat. Once we were done she looked rather majestic, I must admit. If there was a surface on her person that was unadorned, I did not see it. She wore face powder, too. She left with a wide smile, holding on to Mr. Sump's arm, ready to show off.

I hope Mr. Caruso doesn't get blinded by all that magnificence and fall off the stage.

I took her some soup at eight o'clock and she told me she was just going to bed and not to disturb her.

It's odd how families work. Mrs. Sump bullies Lily and snipes at her. Mama and I worked together. We knew what needed to be done and we did it. We all worked in the tavern, we all pitched in because that's the way families work, isn't it?

But there are secrets in this house, and nobody seems to listen to anybody else.

I miss Mama. My heart is aching. I am sorry I shouted at her before I left. I am sorry I didn't kiss her good-bye. I will write to her tomorrow.

APRIL 18, 1906
WEDNESDAY
6:30 A.M.

I never thought I would survive to write this.

My hand shakes and I don't know if I can make the pencil move.

Yet if I don't set it down, if I don't make sense of it—

I must write it so some of the horror can leave me and rest on the page instead.

I am sitting outside of a ruined house. I'm sorry for my handwriting, diary, but I can't seem to stop my trembling.

When I woke at five to my alarm (the clock given to me by Mrs. Sump to make sure I would awaken), the sky was just beginning to lighten to gray. I had gone to bed at two. I was wearing Lily's nightgown but I knew the others would not be up at this hour so I threw a shawl around me and quickly ran down the back stairs to light the fire in the kitchen before I dressed. I had to get the things I'd need to kindle the fires in the bedrooms. While I was in the kitchen I got out the coffeepot, for that was what Mr. Sump preferred, and the tea things. All that was in my head was the list of what Mrs. Sump told me I must do: *fires lit by six, tea at seven in my room, coffee for Mr. Sump in the study, newspapers laid out in dining room, full breakfast at eight thirty.*

I had already lit the coal stove when I heard a noise behind me. Suddenly Lily was in the kitchen, dressed in a plain dark dress and hat—my dress! And carrying my suitcase!

We just stared at each other for a minute, and I saw that she recognized her nightgown on me. And so at the same time we each burst out with questions.

What are you doing in my gown?

What are you doing with my case?

And being that I was the servant I had to answer first, and I told her I had taken the gown to mend — I showed her the tear — but I needed nightclothes because I *thought* my case had been stolen.

And then she looked embarrassed and looked down at the suitcase in her hand. I knew she realized she had no choice but to confide in me.

She said she was leaving, running away. She told me I had to help. She said she'd pay me back, she knew she shouldn't have taken the case with my things, but it was easier to leave as a working girl than to leave as a swell, where they could track her. This way it was a disguise.

"Help me," she said. Her eyes pleaded with me. I'd never seen so much emotion in her face. I realize now that she must have learned to keep her face still and set like a mask to hide what she was feeling from her mother.

"You helped me yesterday," she said. "You knew I left the house."

"I won't spy on you for them," I said. "But this is different."

"All you have to do is say nothing at all. Say you didn't see me."

And I said, "But why are you running away?"

And she smiled, but not like it was directed at me, that smile. She smiled to herself.

She said: "I am running *to* something."

And as she said it the rumble started.

I had a second or two to be confused about the noise. I decided it must be the cable for the cable cars, that maybe they wound it up in the mornings and maybe it rumbled, and so I would feel that underneath the ground every morning and one day it would be a familiar noise.

Just as I decided this, the rumble got louder and became a roar, and then I felt the *power* of it, so terrifying that Lily and I reached out to grab each other but it was as though the house gave a twist and we were thrown away from each other instead.

The noise grew and grew until it was deafening,

like a train was running through the kitchen. The house began to shake with a violence that made Lily and me cry out in terror. Everything in the kitchen — plates, cups, table, chairs, bins, platters, pots, pans — began to shake and shatter. The knowledge roared into my head.

EARTHQUAKE.

So many things happened at the same time that my senses were overwhelmed. Plaster fell, first in a fine cloud and then chunks of it from the ceiling. The floor was moving in a wave but also bumping up and down, making the furniture give great lurches across the floor.

The house was alive. It had us in its jaws and it shook us without mercy. I had one last chance to look into Lily's eyes and I am sure her terror was like my own. I tried to reach for her again but I was thrown backward, right through the doorway into the butler's pantry. I hung on to the door frame as the stove tore loose and danced across the room. To my horror it slammed into Lily and she fell on the floor with a scream. I dropped to my knees and tried to crawl toward her. Part of the ceiling crashed down in front of me and I felt a pain that seemed to burn through me. Clouds of dust suffocated me and I choked and choked, trying to breathe, trying to see.

There seemed to be a pause of a second or two and then the shaking got even worse. Through the haze I saw something incredible, the back wall of the kitchen *moving*. Then the wall fell with a thundering roar — I heard Lily's scream cut short — and I could no longer discern the difference between the bellow of the earth and the clamor of a house coming apart.

Something fell on top of me and the breath was knocked out of me. All was dark. I was sure I was dying.

The shaking stopped. When I opened my eyes I couldn't see anything at first. My eyes stung and my throat was raw. I could move my arms but not my feet. I felt my legs and guessed that I was somehow pinned underneath plaster, but I didn't think my legs were broken because I could wiggle my toes. I was able to get my arms out. I cried for help several times, but that just exhausted me.

Slowly, I wriggled out one arm and began to pick the plaster and bricks off my body. Now that the dust was settling I saw that a chair had fallen over me in such a way that it had saved my life. Chunks of plaster and bricks had fallen, but only a few on me. When I pushed off the chair I was able to sit upright and then wriggle my way out.

My legs were bruised and I had a gash on my ankle and my shoulder, but I was alive.

I flipped over onto my knees. I was face-to-face with the bricks on the floor and I realized that they must be from the chimney. It had crashed straight through the roof.

I raised myself up and saw that the house had cracked like an egg. I saw plaster and wood and tiles, and I couldn't imagine why they were on the kitchen floor. I looked out and saw the pale crescent moon. It was then that I realized that the roof had collapsed.

Did the world split open? That's how it felt. I could hear, faintly, the sound of church bells, and although I knew they were ringing because of the shaking from the quake, had most likely been ringing all along, it felt like they were tolling for the end of the world.

I called for Lily. There was no answer.

I crawled forward and saw her arm, her fingers curled and unmoving. She was covered in bricks and plaster and wood.

The church bells stopped, or maybe the roaring in my ears did, for suddenly it was so quiet. That's what was so odd, after all that crashing and roaring, the quiet was the most absolute I ever heard.

I was afraid to move any farther. I was afraid something would crash on me again. Terror kept me on my knees for long moments.

"Lily!" I whispered. "Please."

Finally I gathered my courage and scrambled over the plaster and bricks and managed to take hold of her hand. There was no answering squeeze.

I began to toss the bricks off, and the chunks of plaster and the wood slats, sobbing and choking, and finally I found her shoulder, and then her face, staring up at me with sightless eyes.

I can't think of it now. If I think of it now, I can't stop seeing it. I'll never stop seeing it, the horror of her staring eyes, and the blood.

I crawled backward and then rose. My legs were shaking. I was afraid to touch anything — a wall, a piece of furniture. I couldn't trust anything anymore, not even the ground underneath me. Nothing was solid anymore, and I wonder if it will ever be again.

On the floor I saw something familiar — the cracked red leather, the faded gold script: RECIPES. I snatched you up, diary, and hugged you. You were the only thing I had to hang on to.

I picked my way back toward the front of the house. The grand draperies had fallen and the front bow window had shaken loose and crashed into the street. I could not get into the parlor, for the chimney had crashed inside the room. In the grand hall the furniture had shifted and some chairs had toppled. Smashed china and glass lay over the floor. The chandelier looked as though it would fall at any moment — I could see the exposed wire. Mrs. Sump's big Chinese vases had smashed. As I passed the study I saw books all over the floor but the ceiling was still intact.

I stopped at the bottom of the staircase, afraid to climb. I tried to call to the Sumps, but my voice was hoarse and cracked and I only choked and coughed instead. I stood there for a moment gathering my courage. Finally I made my legs move. I was afraid of what I might find but I was more afraid that I would have to tell them about Lily.

But I didn't have to tell them.

As I gained the landing and turned, I was able to see to the top of the staircase and I saw Mr. Sump in his nightclothes, his face gray with dust, sitting with his back against the wall. I hurried up the stairs but as I came closer I saw his eyes, staring at me with the ghost of the last great shock of his life. He did not look harmed. It must have been his heart.

He was trying to get to the stairs, that was clear. I tried to get past without looking and nearly kicked his watch, the gold pocket watch he wound with such a satisfied air.

I realized when I turned toward the bedrooms that where the roof and chimneys had fallen at the back of the house was right where Mrs. Sump's bedroom was. She, of course, had the bedroom with the best view.

I stood in the doorway of Mrs. Sump's room and there were bricks and tiles and debris everywhere. The chimney had brought down the roof with it and crashed right through the floor of her room.

Mrs. Sump had made it out of the bed. She was lying on the floor. The massive marble fireplace mantel had fallen on her. She was gone, too.

So they were spared hearing that their daughter was dead, at least.

How was this possible, three lives gone? And mine spared? I couldn't seem to grasp that, I couldn't seem to make sense of the house now, some of the rooms half-buried and some just rearranged.

I was shaking so badly and suddenly so cold. I went into Lily's room. The bed had moved up against the wall and a vase had smashed but she would have survived if she'd been here. I took a dressing gown from her closet and put it around me, tucking you, diary, inside.

And then suddenly the terror came back over me, dropped over my head like a black cloak. What if the house just shrugged its shoulders and came down on top of me? What if the shaking began again?

I ran back down the stairs and outside. I took gulps of the air. My legs gave way and I sat on the lawn.

Destruction around me, chimneys down and things smashed but nothing like the back of a house just falling off, the roof caving in. The Sumps have suffered the worst on this block, at least. There are clouds of dust rising from downtown. A thin plume of smoke. Beyond, the tranquil bay.

And silence. Such silence.

I would have been killed if I'd been in my room. Poor Lily.

I sat there, crying for Lily and holding my journal, and then when the shaking wasn't so bad I untied the string and found the pencil tucked inside, and I wrote this all down.

APRIL 18, 1906
WEDNESDAY
7:15 A.M.

Two hours have passed and I have lived through a lifetime. I have found a place to sit in Union Square while I write this next entry. I am safe here in the open square, gathered with others who have fled their damaged homes. They are mostly poor. The damage has been extensive south of Market Street — south of the Slot, they call it. That's where the cheap rooming houses and hotels and apartments are located. They are fleeing the fires down there. We can see the smoke but we feel quite safe here.

I'm surrounded by people pushing and pulling trunks and carts piled with household goods, anything they could grab by the looks of it, food and quilts and pans and hairbrushes and boots. Some of them are in their nightclothes. I saw a short, stout man in a coat and what looked like pajamas standing there shaking his head, and someone whispered that it was the famous opera singer Enrico Caruso. He left with a few people for the St. Francis Hotel on Powell Street. I hear they are serving breakfast.

There is such a strange mix of the normal and the completely odd. Coffee and rolls while across the square a building's front is gone. I can see rescuers moving through the rooms, looking for survivors. I hear there are people trapped in fallen buildings on Mission Street, still alive, as the fire approaches. I can't think of the poor souls. I hope the firemen can put out the fire soon.

This morning as I sat outside the house immediately after the quake I felt I was the only person alive in the world. Then people began to pour out of their houses, some in their dressing gowns, some obviously dressed hurriedly and missing boots or vests. One woman walked by me with a satin evening cloak thrown over her nightgown. The front of a house down the block had simply fallen off. I could see a bedroom and an easy chair. Bricks and mortar were everywhere. A chimney had fallen on a house next door. Once I looked around I realized that there was not one chimney still standing on the whole block.

A man and a woman walked past, holding the hands of two children, and the children looked solemn and calm. You'd expect them to be crying, wouldn't you? The mother was carrying a birdcage with a parrot in it. The father, a clock. Where they were going, I didn't know at the time, but I imagine they were heading to the waterfront and the ferry.

The city was so quiet. No clang of the cable car, no noise of the streetcar. The sun was rising, and as it rose I could see more clearly that there was a cloud over downtown, hanging in the air, from the collapsed buildings. I heard a rumble and started in fear but realized it must be the noise of a building giving up and collapsing somewhere downtown.

I wondered what the back of the Sumps' house looked like — the part that was now collapsed — but I was afraid to look. I did not want to catch a glimpse of poor Lily again. As it is, the sight of her will live in my mind's eye forever.

An automobile pulled up in front of the house. It was the same Oldsmobile that picked us up from the station. A short man with a beard jumped out and ran to me. He was dressed impeccably in a dark suit and hat, his shirt snowy white. I marveled that he had the presence of mind to dress so carefully on this day. He introduced himself as Mr. Crandall, Mr. Sump's lawyer, and asked if everyone was all right.

It was that simple question that broke whatever hold I had left on my wits. I burst into sobs. I couldn't get any words out. Finally between hiccups I got out some words, strewn like the bricks from the chimney—I couldn't seem to build them into sentences. "Everyone dead," I said. "Roof . . . chimney . . . awful . . ." The sobs were so violent I felt my chest squeezing like a bellows.

"Compose yourself, my dear." He took my handkerchief and pressed it against my face. It came back gray with dust. "Are you sure?" he asked, but I couldn't answer.

He disappeared into the house. When he came out he looked shaken. He said how sorry he was and as soon as he could locate an ambulance or someone he would send them, but of course everyone was still trying to rescue those who were trapped and still living.

Then he noticed the blood on Lily's dressing gown and asked if I was all right, and I said that I just had bruises and scrapes.

He stood looking at me a moment, and I could tell he was thinking hard, trying to devise a plan through all this madness. "You can't stay here," he said. "You'll have to come with me. You'll need to dress," he added, looking away.

Of course I was still wearing Lily's nightgown. I wrapped my arms around myself and rose. My teeth chattered and I realized my bare feet were icy cold: I could barely feel them.

I was afraid to enter the house alone. He said he'd come with me and so I stepped over the threshold once more and began to cry again.

He smoothed his mustache with one hand and then smiled reassuringly. He said he was sure the house was solid but we must hurry. Together we went up the stairs.

Mercifully he had placed a blanket over Mr. Sump.

The attic rooms were wrecked, so I went to Lily's room. I was able to find a shirtwaist and a gray wool skirt trimmed in blue velvet. I took Lily's blue coat, thinking I might need something warm. I found underthings and stockings. Gloves. Lily's boots were a bit too big for me but I pulled them on.

Mr. Crandall called from the landing. "You should pack a bag. You might be away for a while."

The small bag Lily had on the train was still sitting on the window seat. I packed another shirt-waist and a skirt and a few other things. I went to the water closet and turned on the tap but there was no water to wash with. When I looked in the mirror I hardly recognized myself. I found the pitcher of water I'd left by her bed and managed to clean my wounds and scrub off the worst of the dust and blood with a cloth. My braid looked like an old woman's hair, gray and stiff with dust. I used one of Lily's handkerchiefs to wipe it as best I could.

When I came out Mr. Crandall was staring out the window toward downtown. Clouds of dust still hung in the air and I could see thin columns of smoke rising.

"Do you think many buildings collapsed?"

"Only the Lord knows what we'll be dealing with this morning. I need to get to the office downtown. I think it's best you leave the city. My mother lives in Oakland. You can stay there until I get things organized here. I was scheduled to leave on a train on Friday back East. It might be better if you returned to Philadelphia. There's no telling . . ." He stopped, transfixed by what was outside the window, as if he couldn't quite believe it.

Home! My heart sputtered with joy at the thought. I could be home within a week.

"This could be but the prologue. I fear the worst has just begun here," he said.

I could not imagine anything worse than a house almost coming down on top of you.

And he said quietly just one word, very softly, while he stared out at those columns of smoke.

Fire.

We started off down the hill in the auto. I

asked him if his family was all right and he said Mrs. Crandall was quite shaken, but though his chimney had fallen, his house was still intact. After that there was nothing to say. There were no words for what we were seeing.

The streetcar tracks were twisted and had heaved themselves up on the pavement. The surface of the road was buckled, and in some places were holes large enough to swallow the car. Mr. Crandall had to concentrate hard on driving through the debris-strewn street. I saw windows shattered, glass all over the street, and stone moldings and cornices smashed into rubble. A building had collapsed and a horse lay underneath the bricks, dead. A crushed body, just his legs visible, on one corner.

The strange thing is that people were out walking calmly like it was a Sunday. I didn't see any tears or anybody shoving or yelling. They were just walking. When you looked closer you wondered at the assortments of things they carried — a kitten in a pot, a live chicken, a sewing machine, a basket of potatoes with a brocade cushion on top.

"Where are they going?" I asked.

"Same place we are. The ferry."

Some people tried to get Mr. Crandall to take them, offering him money, but he shook his head and just kept driving.

There was a crush of people at the ferry already. One wall of the building looked to be almost completely destroyed, but I could see a line of people waiting.

"Open for business," Mr. Crandall said. "God bless San Francisco."

A mound of baggage — trunks, suitcases, bundles, boxes — were thrown on the pavement as people milled around, waiting for the next boat. Again there didn't seem to be any panic at all. If they spoke, the people spoke quietly. Some of them stood looking down Market Street as if they were stunned and not thinking at all. It had the feeling of a strange dream. If you looked back down Market Street, you saw death and destruction. If you looked at the faces, you wondered if they saw anything at all.

Then the ferry came into sight, chugging across the bay, and the people came alive, surging forward in a great wave of panic.

Mr. Crandall steered through the people trying to cross and came to a halt a few feet down. He put an envelope in my hand with an Oakland address. He thrust a wad of bills in my bag. I told him I couldn't take it but he shook his head impatiently.

"Bribe your way on," he said. "Twenty dollars should do it, start with that but give them more if you have to. I am sorry I cannot escort you. I cannot leave the motor, I have no doubt it will be stolen if I do. And I must get to the office to get the papers out and the accounts. Did you see that fire on Mission Street? It could jump to Market within the hour."

I thanked him, wondering at his great kindness to help a girl he didn't know. I got out of the motor and shut the door. The press of people almost carried me away, but I found my feet.

The auto lurched forward, almost running a young man down.

"Don't worry, Miss Sump! I'll find you!"

I stood there, still as stone as the name clanged inside me.

He thought I was Lily Sump.

I had to stop writing for a moment. I'm feeling so light-headed.

There is a man in the square wearing pink pajamas and a pink bathrobe. He is barefoot. I wonder if I am dreaming.

A woman near me had spread out a cloth and started to feed her family from a basket as though she was picnicking in a park. They were all so calm, even the children, as they ate rolls and drank from their mugs. I went over and offered her five dollars for a roll and a cup of milk. Can you imagine, five dollars for a roll! She was glad to get it. She gave me an apple, too.

My head is clearer now to tell the rest.

I didn't get on the ferry. I stood there for whole minutes while people pushed around me. Now that they were close to their method of escape, they were anxious and some of them were wailing and shouting.

My brain started to work, but slowly, as various thoughts surfaced, as though I was swimming in a thick, oily river and struggling to get my head above water.

Why *wouldn't* he assume I was Lily? I remember him taking my handkerchief to wipe my face — the handkerchief with *L E S* embroidered on the corner. I was wearing a fine nightgown with ribbons and lace. When we came upstairs I went straight to her room and dressed in her clothes.

And when he'd found Lily, she was in the kitchen, dressed in a working girl's clothes.

He had never met her. Never seen a photograph, I suppose. I had overseen the packing of the photographs. There had been one or two of Lily. They were in a trunk in Mrs. Sump's room. I was to have unpacked it today.

All this time, I marveled at the kindness of a man who would rescue a parlormaid. He wasn't. He was rescuing an heiress.

An heiress. Not Minnie Bonner, the maid. Not

the girl whose family had lost everything. Not the girl whose mother was living in a poor rooming house and waiting tables at a tavern not nearly as clean and respectable as the one she'd once proudly owned. Not the daughter of a gambler who had left his family forever.

If he had known who I was, I doubt I would have been standing there so close to safety across the bay. No, I would be one of the countless poor left to find her own way.

He had offered Lily his mother's home, his ticket back East. I couldn't accept it. When the ferry arrived, I watched the people crowd aboard. I watched it leave. Then I turned back to the burning city.

Rumors swirl in the square and are blown like cinders from group to group. Los Angeles has been destroyed. A tidal wave is heading our way. President Teddy Roosevelt is coming to San Francisco personally to see the ruins.

Then there are other rumors that sound more plausible. Someone said there was no water to fight the fires, but how could that be? We are surrounded by water! There is a hydrant on almost every corner. Someone said the fire chief had been badly injured, scalded by steam, and wasn't expected to live.

There are no newspapers to be had, and no news to believe except what is in front of your eyes. With no telephone service and no telegraph, how will the news get out? How will help come?

A woman just walked by me, whispering over and over, "It's the end of the world!"

But it is not the end of me.

As I sat in the square and ate my food the panic started to lift and I could think again.

I looked around me at the chaos and I thought: *Order will come to this place again, but what will happen to me? I will be sent home by Mr. Crandall, if he is kind enough to front me money for a ticket. He will no doubt complete the transaction and sell the tavern. Things like that have a tendency to go on, no matter who is dead.*

I keep thinking about that strongbox.

Inside it is a book full of secrets, and one of

those secrets has to do with how my father was cheated out of his business. And there is money enough to take with me. Nobody but Mr. and Mrs. Sump knows it is there.

Is that stealing? I wonder.

I sat and thought on this for a bit.

First of all, I would be stealing from a thief. Mr. Sump had cheated us.

And was it stealing, if I *was* Lily Sump?

APRIL 18, 1906
WEDNESDAY
NOON

I am back on Nob Hill, and I was wrong. The firemen can't fight the fires because there is no water. South of Market is on fire. The wind is blowing ash and smoke all the way up here. Now I can both see and feel the fires. The air is growing hot.

The first shock this morning was the worst, but not the last. The earth keeps shuddering from time to time, and each time I feel it my whole body responds with panic. Until the shuddering goes away.

When I climbed Nob Hill and got to the house it was still early, I believe before eight o'clock, though it's hard to tell since the clock on the mantel is smashed.

I had to screw tight every nerve to get myself to go inside. I walked through the house with my hands clasped into fists to stop them from shaking. I didn't know if I could climb those stairs again. But I knew what I had to do.

If I could read that ledger, I could read what Mr. Sump's business transactions truly were, and no doubt there would be listed payments to a Mr. Andrew Jewell, and listed next to those payments perhaps what the service was that he rendered. I wasn't sure, but I felt sure enough to think that if I confronted Mr. Crandall with this evidence he might hold back the sale. It might not be too late.

I hesitated on the landing. Mr. Sump still lay at the top. The blanket had slipped off and I could see his face.

I didn't say a prayer. I suppose I should have. I'll say one tonight. But right then, I just tried to understand how someone could be so alive, so full of *force*, and then in an instant or two . . . just something that looked like ash.

My mouth was dry and my hands were icy cold. I bent down and lifted one corner of the blanket, then lifted it a bit more.

I saw his hand, grayish white, on the carpet. Almost as though he were, even in death, still straining to reach for his watch.

For a moment I stood, looking at that hand. I was struck with horror at myself, at what I was about to do.

I did it.

I slid the watch out, clutched it to my chest, and ran, down the stairs and straight to the study. I collapsed on the floor, my back against the desk. My fingers gripped the watch, waiting for my heart to slow down.

When I was calm I turned the watch over in my fingers. At first I was disappointed. There was no key I could discern on the chain. But I examined the ornament — a small lily, with diamond chips — and saw a faint line on the gold backing. I wriggled the backing and it slid forward and fell off into my hand. It was in the shape of a key.

I went to the fireplace where the gilt carvings surrounded the mantel. I tried to remember exactly where Mr. Sump had been standing. I pressed this and that in the wood and nothing happened. The woodwork was intricate here, carved into the shapes of cupids holding up wreaths and laurel leaves and bowls of fruit—it was all so ornate it seemed hideously sinister to me. I pressed one thing and then another and I almost gave up, and then I closed my eyes and thought back to Mr. Sump and tried to remember everything—how he stood, how he moved, what he said.

He said, "my precious flower."

And that's when I saw the fleur-de-lis.

The words in French mean "lily flower," and it is the symbol of the monarchy in France. My father told me about it. He grew up in Lille, in France, and it was on that city's coat of arms.

Mr. Sump's daughter was his precious flower.

There was only one fleur-de-lis in the tangle of gilt leaves. I pressed it and the hidden panel slid open.

I reached inside for the strongbox. I shut the panel, then walked to the desk and put the metal box down. I placed the flat key in the odd-shaped lock and turned it, and it opened.

Laid on top of the neatly stacked bundles of cash was a ledger. I took out the ledger and shook out the cash. It was impossible to tell how much it was — there were five stacks of hundred-dollar bills.

I was more interested in the ledger. Holding it in my hands, I took a seat at the desk.

That's when the aftershock hit. I heard the rumble and now I knew what it was. This wasn't like the small shakes and bumps of the morning. This had enough power to terrify. The house shook. The lamp in the corner crashed to the floor. I managed to get the ledger and strongbox and crawled underneath the desk, hanging on for dear life.

It was not a long shake, but it was a hard one.

The chandelier over my head creaked and swung, the glass pendants making a noise like music without notes. The desk gave a final heave and I bumped up against it, banging my head.

The shaking stopped.

I poked my head out from underneath the desk. Some of the glass globes of the chandelier had crashed to the floor. A crystal vase that had survived the initial quake had finally given up and toppled down from a shelf. The secret panel had popped open — I guess because I hadn't shut it properly — and I saw something gray poking out. I went over and withdrew a cloth sack. It had been shoved to the very back of the compartment. This time when I closed the compartment door I locked it. I took the bundle over to the desk and shook it. A stack of papers slid out. I guessed they were some sort of certificates. On the top paper I saw the words BEARER BOND and BACKED BY GOLD and the amount: $10,000.

There looked to be a stack about two inches thick. I riffled through them and they all seemed to be for the same amount. I wasn't sure what that meant, or what a "bearer bond" was. I started to add up the totals but I got lost in zeroes. I realized these had to be worth hundreds of thousands of dollars.

I took the sack and placed it in the bottom of the strongbox, then stacked the cash on top. All of it wouldn't fit so I put some back in the safe. Then I sat down and opened the ledger again.

I was disappointed to discover it was just amounts and names, and I didn't know the names and what they meant. In tiny writing at the top of one page was written "SF Board of Supervisors" and then a list of names and amounts. Bribes, I guessed. A notation read "Home Telephone Co." And next to it an address of a wire factory. Then a notation about the "United Railroads" and more lists of amounts and names. It seemed amazing to me that Mr. Sump would write down such a long list of bribes, but then again, how else could he keep track of it? There were so many.

On one page was written "Arthur Langley,

$5,000," but it was crossed out. So that was the source of the feud, I suppose.

I flipped back a few pages and found some Philadelphia notations, names of streets surrounding the tavern. Under the street address of our tavern was written the name of one of the Philadelphia city supervisors and "$3,000." So he had bribed people back there, too. I remembered inspectors coming around, more than usual last year. Once they threatened to close the place, but my mother fought it and won.

Then I saw the name Andrew Jewell. There were three payments of a thousand dollars each and then a final payment of three thousand. The date was January 25. It was only a month later that Mr. Sump gave us an eviction notice.

There was more — addresses of buildings bought and sold. Records of other transactions. Account numbers. The name of the San Francisco mayor, a date a week from now, and amounts with question marks.

I wasn't sure exactly what I held in my hands

but I knew one thing: Mr. Sump had been a crook. I had a feeling this little book could have put Mr. Sump in jail for a long time, had he lived.

Did Mr. Crandall know? I didn't think so. I couldn't imagine that kind man from this morning helping to destroy a family in Philadelphia, paying bribes to politicians.

I slid the ledger back into the strongbox. The question was where to hide it. It was too heavy for me to carry very far.

I would have to hide it here and plan what to do. But where? As I sat and thought, I heard footsteps out in the main hall.

There was no time to put the strongbox back behind the wall. I ran as quietly as I could to the sofa and shoved it underneath. Then I tiptoed out into the hallway. The footsteps were heading toward me, and in another moment Mr. Crandall came around the corner, walking quickly. He no longer looked like the perfectly dressed attorney in a dark suit and hat from this morning. His clothes were covered in ash and spotted with tiny burn holes. He gave a start when he saw me.

"Miss Sump! What are you doing here? I put you on the ferry."

"I couldn't get on, so—"

He brushed past me and went into the study, still talking. He began to go through the desk. With every phrase he opened another drawer, looked inside, and shut it with a bang. I could not get a word in if I tried.

"Then you should have waited for the next one! You could have been safe across the bay. Now I shall have to look after you, too." BANG.

"There's no telling how badly this will go." BANG.

"The Army has arrived downtown and is patrolling, but looters will be out I am sure. Another fire has started in Hayes Valley." BANG.

"If the fires join, the entire downtown could be up in flames, and part of the Western Addition, too." BANG.

"Do you understand? There's no water. The water mains are broken!" BANG.

He turned to me, rising on his toes and back down again, as if to make himself taller as he delivered his pronouncement.

"Lily — if I may call you that — I am your guardian now. You are my ward. I drew up your father's will myself. You are the only heir, and my responsibility. The money will all go into a trust, which I will administer until you are twenty-one. Forgive me for speaking of this now, but . . ." He ran his hand through his hair and it came back streaked with gray. He stared at it.

"Circumstances demand it. I barely got the records out in time. But your father . . . he removed something from the office safe. I don't know where it is. But your future may depend on it. There is a ledger — a record of our business. Perfectly legitimate, I assure you." He smoothed his mustache. "It will help me to continue as he would have wished in the next few weeks. See to all his business. Did you ever see him with it?"

I hesitated, but he barely waited for my response. He turned around and examined the room, his gaze roaming while he spoke.

"Do you know where he would keep important papers? There were also bonds — almost a million dollars in bonds, Lily. *I can't find them.* Do you know if he has a safe?"

I don't think he even expected an answer. He began to go through the bookshelves, looking behind the books and opening them, then returning them to the shelves.

He started calmly enough. But he quickly grew frenzied, pulling books from the shelves and tossing them to the floor. Soon the shelves were empty.

This was the moment I should have confessed, diary. I admit it!

But I remained silent. There was something so wild in his eyes. There could be only one explanation for his frenzy — he knew about those columns of bribes in the ledger. He was a crook, too.

The lie was so enormous I couldn't believe I could tell it. Every time he had said *Lily* it was like a hammer against my breastbone.

But if there was a chance to save my family, I had to take it.

He ran upstairs to Mr. Sump's bedroom and I

heard things crashing up there as well. But when he came downstairs he was calmer.

"I will just have to search again," he said. "If I cannot find them, it is unlikely that a looter will. Don't worry." He smoothed his mustache and smiled. "I only have your best interests at heart. You are well protected."

That's when I realized: the smoothing of the mustache, the false smile. That was his tell. That's what he did when he lied.

Which meant he didn't have Lily's best interests at heart. . . .

Suddenly a loud blast split the air, and I jumped. He told me that the Army under the direction of General Funston was starting to dynamite buildings to create a firebreak. If the fire couldn't feed on something, it would die.

"That's good, then," I said.

"Unless as the buildings go up the wind takes the embers and the next building catches fire."

I looked out and saw the trees moving, the wind fluttering the branches. It was an ominous sight.

"We are safe up here," he said. "There is plenty of space between there and here."

"Mr. Crandall," I said. "I was wondering . . . I know that this is a perilous time, and decisions will no doubt have to made later, but . . . I keep thinking of poor Minnie. The maid," I added, because he looked blank. "Minette Bonner. In light of what happened, I would like to give something to the family. When this is over. I'd like them to have their business back."

"How do you know about this? Did the maid tell you?"

"She did mention it to me."

"Well. I don't want you to worry about such things. We can't just forgive debts." He chuckled. "This is why you need a guardian, Lily. A young girl has sentimental ideas and the next thing you know, you're in the poorhouse. No," he said soothingly, "let me take care of the business. You needn't concern yourself."

I tried to argue, but he wasn't listening to me at all.

"You need company and protection right now.

So you'll have to come to my house on Green Street and stay with Mrs. Crandall. We should take your mother's jewels, at least. You don't have to enter that room again. Can you direct me?"

"The diamonds she wore last night are still on her dresser," I said. "The rest she keeps in a small red case. It is in the drawer of her dressing table." After the words left my mouth I wondered if it would seem suspicious. I answered as a maid would answer, not a daughter.

He didn't notice. "Mrs. Crandall will be worried. I'll take you over to Russian Hill. The car has been commandeered by the Army. We have to walk."

He went up the stairs while I waited below, and then we walked out with our pockets stuffed with jewels. The air was thick and smoky. Ash and cinders drifted down on us, a dark, silent snow.

APRIL 18, 1906
WEDNESDAY
MIDNIGHT

I am at the Crandall residence on Green Street. I am awake, we are all awake. Because of the smoke and the fires it was dark early — six o'clock. No one feels comfortable indoors. We sit outside on the living room furniture Mr. Crandall has dragged from the house with the help of the neighbors. We'll spend the night outside here on this small patch of lawn. There is too much danger that cinders and sparks could land on the roof and the house will go up. All the neighbors are out and some have dragged furniture to sit on the lawn with us. We are all keeping watch.

When we arrived Mrs. Crandall pounced on her husband, demanding to know why he was gone so long. She is his height, but round and puffy-looking, and she hung on his arm while she talked. You could tell he wanted to shake her off and just sit down. He explained that the streets are sometimes impassable and he was almost caught in the fire when he went to check on Mr. Sump's properties on Mission Street. He had tried to help rescue people from a collapsed building but the fire came too close.

Mrs. Crandall said she was out of her mind with worry and then finally noticed me. When Mr. Crandall introduced me she instantly swiveled, pushed at her hair, and offered me tea that, it turned out, she could not provide.

Then I saw what it was like to be not only rich, but the source of somebody's income. As the heir, Lily Sump held this family's fortune in her hands.

I would be untruthful, diary, if I said I did not enjoy this a bit.

She found me a chair and a glass of water (how precious water is to us now! I shared it with a neighbor who came by) and has been so solicitous of my comfort, even while not being able to offer me any comfort at all.

The sky is orange with the flames, and they have been dynamiting to create firebreaks. We are almost used to the blasts now.

As the night wore on Mrs. Crandall directed Mr. Crandall to fetch this or that from the house, just in case we have to evacuate. I don't understand how she thinks we can transport all these trunks, clothes, and bedding without a car or a horse and carriage. I realized that she looked puffy because she is wearing two dresses and a shirtwaist and I don't know how many petticoats. She doesn't want to leave her best gowns behind.

We are several blocks east from Van Ness Avenue. West of Van Ness, they say, is not on fire. Mr. Crandall said they will try to use Van Ness as a firebreak since it is a wide avenue. So if we have to walk away, we don't have far to go. The Army will tell us when to leave.

It seems as though the entire city is walking. The people carry all kinds of things, chairs and phonographs and pets, or walk by pushing baby carriages and children's wagons piled with clothing and groceries and footstools and paintings. I saw one person who had attached wheels to a stove and was pushing it with difficulty down the street.

Even with my eyes closed I hear the *scrape, scrape* of trunks being dragged. It is the most mournful sound I have ever heard.

Many are heading all the way to Golden Gate Park or the Presidio. There are supplies there, and nurses. Some head to the open squares.

No one in San Francisco is allowed to light a stove. The soldiers came by with the order. We heard that the fire in Hayes Valley, the one that caused City Hall to burn, was caused by someone cooking breakfast in a stove with a broken chimney. Mr. Crandall's neighbor brought us some apples and hard-boiled eggs for our supper, and Mrs. Crandall shared the corned beef her cook had made for supper the night before. Her cook went to check on her family in the Mission District and has not returned. The driver went to look in on his sister. Mrs. Crandall has done nothing but complain about how disloyal both servants are. It seems to me she would have gotten along with Mrs. Sump. When I told her this she took it as a compliment.

Earlier in the afternoon Mr. Crandall walked to a meeting called by the mayor of some of the important men in San Francisco and was gone for hours. While he was gone the air got hotter and we began to hear the flames, a dull steady roar. Mrs. Crandall moaned over and over that he was surely dead, until I thought I would scream. She spoke to a neighbor who said "the Italians" cleared the store of everything they could load in a wagon and left. Mrs. Crandall said they should be arrested and that's what the city gets for taking in so many immigrants. It took me a while to understand that they were talking about the Jennardi family grocery. Mrs. Crandall said, "Oh, that family! Running all over that store . . . all those children, I can't tell one from another."

I had forgotten about Jake.

What if I am here and he comes by and identifies me as Minnie? Apparently the family has taken off to safety, but once the fires are gone they will return. He could expose me.

Whatever I am going to do, I must do it before he returns.

His map is still tucked into the pages of the diary. I take it out and study it — the bold quick lines of Van Ness, the X where the Sump mansion is, the X where the Jennardi grocery is, downtown,

City Hall, the long rectangle of Golden Gate Park. I can see now where the fire is and why Mr. Crandall is concerned. We will be surrounded by fire on three sides and our backs will be to the bay.

Now that I understand the geography, I have a little more respect for Mrs. Crandall's panic.

When Mr. Crandall returned, the neighbors gathered to hear his news. He told of the buildings that were gone and with each name came a gasp and a moan from the crowd. City Hall, he said, was just a shell. The Call Building had burned, and the Palace Hotel.

"Not the Palace!" Mrs. Crandall cried. "It is fireproof!"

Mr. Crandall said that if he's learned anything today it is that nothing is fireproof. There is a dedicated group trying to save the Mint, he said, and the postal workers are staying to fight the fire at the Post Office. But the fire has spread in a new direction. Chinatown is almost burned out.

The fire had jumped past Stockton Street now and they were making a stand at Powell. Everyone gasped and I realized I had been at Powell Street that morning—it ran alongside Union Square, where we had all felt so safe. I asked him about the St. Francis Hotel and he shook his head.

"If they don't halt it at Powell and Sutter, it could go up Nob Hill," he said.

At that the faces got that set look that means people are scared. That meant that the fire could come at Russian Hill from two directions.

Mr. Crandall took me aside and told me in a solemn voice that he had arranged for Mr. and Mrs. Sump and Lily (only he called her "the maid") to be taken to the temporary morgue in the Presidio. I feel so much better now that I don't have to think of them still lying in that house.

Mrs. Crandall wants us to evacuate—she says Mr. Crandall should find a cart, and we should go to her sister's house in Eureka Valley, which is south and west of us. It is still in the city but safe from the fires, so far. Mr. Crandall said aside from the difficulty of securing a conveyance—for the Army and police have confiscated everything they can get to help the wounded and to fight the fires—she hasn't spoken to her sister in five years, ever since she married an Irishman. What makes her think her sister will take them in?

Diary, between the Irish and the Italians and the Chinese and the Japanese, Mrs. Crandall is running out of groups to look down on.

What would she say if she knew I was the daughter of a tavern owner, my mother with Irish blood and my father an immigrant? I am nothing but a mongrel.

Mrs. Crandall says that family is family and blood is blood. Mr. Crandall said she once said she would never forgive her sister.

Mrs. Crandall said that was before she was sitting in the middle of the devil's cauldron.

APRIL 19, 1906
THURSDAY
2 A.M.

I can't sleep. When I close my eyes, all I see is fire.

The smoke is shot through with an orange glow. The fires have joined and there is one fire now, miles long, they say. The city is destroying itself around us. We hear the dynamite and then the thunderous roar of collapse. Wood and stone become dust, which rises in the air and mingles with the smoke.

Mr. Crandall has gone again, this time to see if the perimeter of the fire has moved, and where it is. He will walk to Van Ness and see if he can learn whether we must walk to Eureka Valley tonight or if we can wait until morning.

The lawn is now even more crowded with neighbors who have dragged chairs and blankets here. The men are talking of staying, of fighting the fire that is coming, of not letting their houses be dynamited. You can see that Mrs. Crandall doesn't like all this company but I would think she'd be glad.

How will they fight? There is no water. Somebody spoke of looking for cisterns that have been forgotten. Someone else suggested gathering all the vinegar from their homes, and blankets to snuff out sparks.

They say things like, *I won't abandon my home* or, *I can't leave Mother's dining table*, but yet, what will they do when the fire comes? It is now an inferno. It is so powerful that it makes its own wind, a wind that seems to suck out what we need to live and give us only heat, only ash.

LATER

Just now a family walked by who said they were coming down from Nob Hill. Nob Hill will go within the hour, they said.

Mrs. Crandall is asleep. Mr. Crandall is talking to a group of men in the street.

I should have buried the strongbox. That's what the people here are doing, burying their valuables in case the fire comes.

It's my only hope to have a life if I survive this.

Diary, I am afraid. I have to go back to the Sump house one more time.

LATER
6 A.M.

The grass is scorched. When I run my finger along it, it comes up black.

In the early hours of the morning I left the Crandall home and started up Jones Street. It was a long walk, and fatigue had settled in my bones.

I trudged up the hill against the stream of people coming down. Some of them warned me that Nob Hill was not safe any longer. I kept going.

When I got to Sacramento Street I stopped to look around me. What had sometimes seemed like a dream over the past hours was suddenly too real. The sky was lit with fire. It was beautiful and terrible, like something outside of the world I'd always known. The wildness and fierceness of the fire drove the wind, and it shimmered with heat. The pavement was hot beneath the soles of my boots.

I ran to the Sump house. We hadn't bothered to lock the door since anyone could get in through the shattered bay window. Inside the house I ran through rooms illuminated by the flames. I reached the study and fell to my knees in front of the sofa. When I found the strongbox I sobbed in relief.

There was a small carpet in front of the fireplace. I staggered over with the box and placed it there. I knew I would only be able to carry the box a few feet. I dragged the carpet through the study, down the long hallway, and pulled my burden out the front door.

I was suddenly seized with fear that the shovel would be gone — stolen by a passerby. But there it was, lying on the ground next to the overturned barrel and the slate tiles from the roof.

I started to dig. It was hard, hot work. My sore shoulder ached terribly, and it felt as though I was breathing smoke and fire. When I heard soldiers I dived down behind the stone wall until they passed.

I felt something burn my arm and I swatted away a spark. When I looked up I saw licks of flame on the roof of the Sump mansion. Smoke trailed from an attic window.

Fear drove me then. I dug frantically, as if my life depended on it. I heard a roar at my back but I didn't turn, I just kept digging until the hole was deep enough to hold the strongbox. When I judged the strongbox could fit in the hole with a few inches of dirt over it, I dragged it and pushed it inside. I quickly patted the earth down over it and then found a few bricks to place over the dirt to mark the spot.

I heard the sound of popping, and suddenly glass rained down. The windows of the house were exploding from the heat. I felt glass in my hair.

I ran to the street, but when I reached it I turned back for one last look at the house. The wind must have picked up then, for the smoke clouds, a mile high in the sky, shifted and scudded away for a moment and the pale moonlight shone down. I saw flickering shadows in an attic window, and caught sight of a line of fire on a curtain. The fire seemed almost lazy, taking its time with licks and feints, but I knew that when it unleashed, the mansion would go quickly. There was so much to burn.

I turned to look up at the crown of the hill. I saw sparks on the roof of the fireproof Fairmont Hotel. It would burn. It would all burn. The millionaires couldn't escape the fire after all.

A group of firemen suddenly appeared, walking down Jones Street. They gave me a start. Covered in gray ash, they looked like ghosts. When they saw me, one of them gestured. I could see the urgency in his expression even though I could also see that he was too exhausted to lift his arm all the way.

"What are you doing up here?" one of them bellowed at me as I came closer. "Nob Hill is going!"

"I'm on my way to Russian Hill to stay with my guardian," I answered.

"You'd better walk with us, miss," one of them said. "They've been giving out badges and guns too freely. Men happy to shoot at what they think is a looter and no questions asked."

"It's hard to believe that folks would take advantage in this sort of calamity," a young fireman said, and the others laughed tiredly.

"You think so, Patrick?" one said kindly. "You haven't been working long enough, then."

"Well, one got his comeuppance down on Montgomery," another said. "Trying to steal a safe from a burned-out wreck. He pried it open and poof! All the cash went up in smoke. You'd only have to look around you to know that oxygen feeds fires. You'd think he'd have more sense."

"Speaking of which, look at our General Funston. Who put him in charge, I'd like to know. Using black powder to blow up buildings. He's causing half the trouble."

"Need a firebreak, though."

"Ain't going to get one if he doesn't stop making things worse."

"If only the Chief were here. Tully was down at the hospital earlier, said he's bad off."

"If only they listened to him about the mains. Wouldn't be trying to fight fires with dirt and cistern water."

"It'll be the end of the world if the Navy doesn't get here," one said.

An older fireman snorted. "If they can help. We'll have to look mighty sharp to connect our hoses with theirs — no telling if we can get a hose line going. Otherwise they'll sit in the bay and throw salt water at the waterfront."

"Do you think the whole city could burn?" I asked.

That stopped their talk. One of them started

to say something, some words of reassurance, but he couldn't get them out.

The only answer was the sound of our footsteps heading down the hill.

They split off from me at Broadway, heading west, they said, to Van Ness. They advised me to do the same — to head west in the morning.

When I got to the Crandall house, I saw that Mrs. Crandall had dropped off to sleep on the sofa on the lawn. Mr. Crandall slept in the armchair, facing the flames of Nob Hill.

I sat on the lawn, hugging my knees, and looked back from where I'd come. I watched the glow in the sky arc and brighten. The mansions of the rich were burning. I could hear the ferocious roar of the fire as it moved.

Suddenly I missed Mama so badly I could hardly breathe. If I could only go back and change our last meeting. I didn't even kiss her good-bye. She had no doubt heard of the earthquake by now. What was she thinking?

And Papa. I wish that we had said good-bye. That was a word he never used.

He always knew when he was leaving. Why didn't he ever say good-bye?

He would come home and lift me up and kiss me. For that one moment, I would have his full attention. I would think — he's gone away and now he's back, now he knows how much he loves us.

How much did he love us?

I felt as though I couldn't keep my eyes open a second longer. I wondered how long I would walk that day and where I would go. My feet ached in my too-big boots and my chest hurt when I took a breath, and I was sitting with strangers on the cold ground. I had no comfort and no home anymore. Who was I now? I wasn't Lily Sump, but I didn't feel like Minnie Bonner anymore, either. Whoever I had been was gone. I was no one.

I had walked into another life, at first by accident, and then by design. What if I became Lily Sump for good? I could have more money than I ever dreamed. I would never worry about anything again. And people would wait on *me*.

If I were Lily Sump, I could get on a ship and

go anywhere. I could go to Paris. Mr. Crandall would make me hire a companion, but I would be in charge. Being in charge means that you are the one with the money.

Wouldn't it be easier for Mama if I just disappeared? She could mourn the daughter who died in the quake and never worry about her again. I could send her money somehow, make up a story about a long-lost relative. At least I'd know she was safe and comfortable. I couldn't do that as Minnie, but I could if I were a Sump.

I fell asleep thinking of silks and satins, warm blankets and soft beds.

LATER
1 P.M.

It is a battle we are living through.

When General Funston could not bring down buildings with dynamite, he used artillery. His object was to bring down every building on the east side of Van Ness. All day we've heard the crashing and booming and felt that strange push against our eardrums that meant another explosion had occurred. Glass is all over the streets as the windows shatter from the concussions.

Thousands of people are gathered at the bottom of Van Ness, at the edge of the bay. They hope to escape by sea.

The good news is that the Navy ships have arrived. They have set up a system to bring salt water to the fire. I don't know if it is working. At any rate the hoses will not reach here. I remember what the firemen said about the difficulty of connecting the hoses.

It has been a day of dithering. Mr. Crandall wants to stay and stand with the neighbors who vowed not to leave their homes even when the Army ordered them to vacate. They leave and they come back. They are determined to save Russian Hill, or at least the crown of the hill. The neighbors I had met last night, the Livermores and the Putnams, are staying. There is a cistern they can use for water. They have only towels and carpets to fight the flames. They are determined.

Mrs. Crandall begged her husband to leave. In the battle between the roaring inferno and Mrs. Crandall, Mrs. Crandall proved stronger.

We are carrying all that we can and leaving the house behind.

LATER
5 P.M.

We are here in Lafayette Square, just a few blocks west of Van Ness. The square is crowded with people, but you've never heard such a silence. We stand on the crown of this hill, and we look east at the fire.

All afternoon the sky was all smoke. We saw the fire spread from one house to another. There were no tears. Only awe. We are at the fire's mercy now. There is no stopping it.

APRIL 20, 1906
FRIDAY
7 A.M.

We woke to the same red sky.

After a breakfast of a stale roll and some cheese washed down with cider, Mrs. Crandall said we must leave today. There is no chance we can get across the firebreak of Van Ness back to the house, even if she wanted to.

Early this morning the fire reached Franklin Street, which is only a block from us. They fought it and won.

Thousands and thousands of refugees are moving, as far as I can see, thick as ants, some still heading down toward the bay. Some go west toward the ocean.

I think I would feel better with the sea at my back, but Mrs. Crandall insists on going to her sister's.

Mr. Crandall is reluctant to leave. He says we're safe here for now. But the fire is too close for Mrs. Crandall.

He is going to try to walk closer to Van Ness, closer to the fire, although he suspects he will get chased away by the soldiers. He is anxious to know if all of Russian Hill is going.

I asked to accompany him and he said it would be all right. I am just as anxious for news. I will report back.

Diary, I hardly know what to think. Just now I walked over to Van Ness with Mr. Crandall. While he spoke to someone escaping from the fire on Russian Hill, I hung back, watching a group of men being rounded up by several soldiers who needed them to carry hoses. From what I could see, they want to connect the fire department hoses with the hoses from the Navy ships at the foot of Van Ness so that they can use salt water to fight the fire.

Some of the men were not happy to pause in their flight to assist them, but the soldiers pointed their rifles and the men agreed quickly.

One of the men stood out with his air of elegance, despite the fact that he was dressed like the rest of us in sooty clothes, his white shirt grimy with ash and his beard dark with sweat. His derby was pushed to the back of his head, revealing his dark blond hair. I recognized him immediately.

It was Andrew Jewell.

"Lily!" Mr. Crandall called to me, and in that strange occurrence that can sometimes happen, the world seemed to go completely silent for a moment — no dynamiting, no shouts — and as I turned to Mr. Crandall, Andrew Jewell turned as well. He saw me, and his gaze moved from me to Mr. Crandall. He stood for a long moment, holding the hose, and we locked eyes. I felt his gaze on me as I took Mr. Crandall's arm and we started back along the sidewalk.

My mind buzzed with questions. Had he heard Mr. Crandall call me Lily? If he had, he had hid whatever surprise he felt. He didn't raise a cry of greeting.

Why did his gaze linger so long on us? As though he knew exactly what I was doing. As though he saw my scheme.

They are calling me. We'll press on to Eureka Valley. I will be glad to leave Mr. Jewell behind.

But now I know that there is someone in this city who knows who I am, and where I came from.

My father's enemy, and mine.

APRIL 21, 1906
SATURDAY
11 A.M.

I have so much to report! It helps to write to you, diary. When all is confusion, I can look back and see what happened when. Even though I can't puzzle out the *why* sometimes of what I do.

Yesterday morning, we walked and walked, carrying our bundles. Even Mrs. Crandall grew too tired and overwhelmed to complain. At one point we passed through where the fire had raged, and I caught sight of City Hall in the distance, smoking and wrecked, its bare dome now just twisted metal, looking rather like one of the birdcages I had seen carried over the past days.

As we circled south to avoid the fires that were still advancing on Mission Street, Mr. Crandall found a horse and cart that for a fee agreed to transport us to Eureka Valley. The driver had just come from the area and was bringing back supplies of food for the exhausted firemen. We climbed among sacks of cooked hams and apples and canned beans.

The going was not easy, with the pavement so torn and buckled, and there were several times that the driver had to stop completely, as landmarks such as street signs and buildings had simply disappeared. It was also slow going because the horse was so tired, and the driver told us he was looking forward to "giving poor Charlie a rest."

He pointed down Valencia Street, which looked badly torn up. There was a large fissure in the pavement of the street and the houses looked crooked, some leaning over the street in an alarming fashion. I saw a large hotel sitting squat on the ground, and he explained that the hotel used to be four stories, and had collapsed during the quake, flattening like a pancake, with many trapped inside. People on the fourth floor merely had a hard jolt and simply stepped out onto the street. The others, he said, were not so lucky. Passersby were able to rescue a few, but the rest perished. The thought of that horror kept us silent for several blocks.

When the carriage got to Dolores Street and Market, our driver was hailed by a friend who came racing up, waving his arms.

"We need you, Will!" he cried.

"Well, can't you see I'm coming?" our driver answered with some annoyance in his tone, for he really had been traveling as quickly as he could. "I've got the food in the back, just giving these people a lift up the hill."

"Well, they'll have to get out and walk, then," the young man said.

"We will do no such thing!" declared Mrs. Crandall.

"What's the problem, Mike?" our driver asked.

"The fire has broken through Mission and is almost on us. If it takes us here it will go full west. We'll lose the whole city. We have a chance to stop it. We've got the firemen and the trucks at the bottom of the hill, and we've got a fire hydrant on Church and Twentieth that's working, by Jove! But we can't get the fire truck to the hydrant. The poor horses are almost dead from the work they've done and they just can't pull it."

"What are you proposing to do?"

"We're going to push the thing up the hill

to Twentieth Street, what else?"

"Push the fire trucks up that hill? You must be daft!"

"It'll be a job, that's for certain! We've got hundreds of men up at Mission Park and more coming every minute, pouring in from all over the Mission and the hills and the valley, too. Shoulder to shoulder we'll be with the firemen, poor exhausted devils. We've got carpets and brooms and shovels, and we're going to stamp out every spark. We've got water, thank the Lord, and we're going to use it. We're going to fight the fire here and not give up until it goes out."

Such simple words, spoken from a man streaked with dirt, a man not much older than a boy. But something about the way he said it thrilled me.

For two days we had run from the fire. And here was a chance to meet it and conquer it.

I discovered something at that moment, diary. If you see enough destruction, if you feel helpless in the face of it, if you've been terrified enough times, there does come a moment when you cannot bear one more thing to be lost. I was tired of being afraid. Tired of moving *away* from the fire. I wanted to fight.

"We've got to help," I said to Mr. Crandall.

"No, Hugh," Mrs. Crandall said. "I will not allow it! You're not a young man. And you cannot send me up to my sister with only Miss Sump. Who knows what could happen? We need an escort."

"I want to stay," I said, but they were not listening to me.

Our driver turned. "Sorry, folks, but you'll have to get off here. Follow this street down to Noe and head straight up the hill. I'm going to head to Mission Park."

"You most certainly are not!" Mrs. Crandall sputtered. "We paid you for a ride to my sister's!"

"Here's your money, then," the driver said, handing it back. "And if you won't get out, I'll toss you out myself." He eyed Mr. Crandall. "We sure could use another man to help, though. Didn't you hear?"

I could see Mr. Crandall hesitate. He didn't want to look like a coward.

"You heard him, Hugh — they have hundreds of men to help," Mrs. Crandall said. "What is more important — your wife and your ward, or a fire that cannot be stopped with the addition of just one extra man?"

"Ah," Mr. Crandall said, "that describes me in your eyes, doesn't it, my dear. Just one extra man."

I almost felt sorry for him then.

Slowly, Mr. Crandall swung himself down. He reached up for his wife and helped her down. Then me. I tossed down our bundles before I stepped off.

Mr. Crandall must have seen what I was thinking in my face. "They will not let a young woman help," he said. "It would do no good for you to go in any event."

But he was wrong. I knew I could prove him wrong. What am I but what a boy is — with arms to fetch and carry, with legs to run?

So I dropped my bundles and my suitcase, and as they turned to go and the driver urged his horse and the cart began to move, I picked up my skirts and hoisted myself into the back once more.

By the time the Crandalls turned, startled to see I wasn't with them, I was halfway down the block.

I jumped off the cart as we reached Mission Park and joined the stream of people running, walking, trudging, because we were all headed to the same destination for the same purpose — to fight.

I don't know what I expected Mission Park to be, but it was hardly a park, just a long rectangle of dirt that stretched for blocks up the hill. It was filled with refugees and I could see the exhausted horses, their heads drooping, standing on one corner.

I was back close to the fire again, and the sound of it was a continuous roar. The smoke was terrible. At first I couldn't make sense of what I was seeing. It seemed like chaos.

But it wasn't, not quite. As I hurried up the hill on the Church Street side I saw that the firemen were already at the top of the hill. There was a gang of men with their shoulders against the fire truck, another on the sides, and still more pulling ropes. Slowly they were getting that truck up the hill. I could hear their shouts as they egged one another on to keep going.

I could see the hot orange of sparks in the smoky air, and cinders as big as my fist were raining down from the sky. The fire was blazing to the east of us and some of the houses on Dolores were already starting to smolder and burn.

Then I saw that men stood on the roofs of the buildings trying to snuff out the flames with rugs and towels. They were in the yards and on the porches. They were beating out flames. The heat was so intense that within minutes they would be overcome, but others immediately stepped up to take their place. There were hundreds and hundreds of people, maybe more, more than my eye could see, along the fire line. The dynamiting was still going on, and the sound of it was pressure against my ears.

Suddenly through the roar of the fire and the shouting I heard a voice calling.

"Philadelphia!"

It was Jake Jennardi. I barely recognized him.

A scarf was tied around his mouth and his face was black with soot. His cap was singed.

"What are you doing here?" he shouted. "It's not safe!"

"I want to help!"

"We got the steamer up the hill," he said, his voice raspy with smoke and excitement. He pointed at the fire truck. "We've set up a relay of the hoses, we got water, and we'll get it pumping. Hot dog! We're just beating out the sparks and we're filling milk cans to pour on the roofs. We're going to save the neighborhood, we'll do it! We've torn off some doors from the houses and we're holding them up for the firemen, to protect 'em, and when they get too hot, we hose 'em down."

"What can I do?"

"You can help fill the milk jugs, I reckon. My ma and my sister Beatrice are a couple blocks over, setting up a food and aid station for those that pass out—we carry 'em over."

"Take me there," I told him. And that was how I got in the thick of it, fighting the last fire of the San Francisco quake.

I don't remember falling asleep. I do remember falling down somewhere before dawn, right on the dirt of Mission Park. Which I have discovered is mixed with manure. They were about to plant the grass when the quake struck.

Well, it made a soft bed, and I couldn't afford to be choosy.

I think one of the Jennardis put a blanket over me, because now I have it to hold around my shoulders.

The fire is out.

All is black and smoking. Soot and muck. But the fire is out.

I can see from here, at the top of the park, the ruined city. San Francisco is a city tossed and broken, but from what I saw last night, it will survive.

I think I must have met a dozen Jennardis last night. Jake; his brother, Joseph; his sister, Beatrice; his cousin Robert; several cousins whose names I did not catch; his uncle Angelo, his mother and father; his aunt . . . and a baby called Rose.

People are lying all around me, exhausted from

last night. Thousands were on the streets, helping to fight the fire. Thousands of hands, beating at the flames, thousands of boots, stamping on the cinders.

My name over the course of the past twenty-four hours has been shortened from "Philadelphia" to "Philly," and now I am merely "Phil" to the Jennardis.

"Phil, bring another jug, will you?"

"Phil, can you hold the baby?"

Honestly, diary, I do not know who I am anymore. But I know I feel safe with the Jennardis. I wish . . . I don't know what I wish. We have been too busy to really talk, but I wish I could tell Jake about the spot I'm in. About how I let Mr. Crandall think I was Lily. About the strongbox and the ledger and how I want to save my family and how I was tempted to *be* Lily because it just seemed easier to have money than not.

And how seeing those firemen drag themselves up that hill when they were exhausted, seeing the steam rise off their rubber coats, seeing the heat overtake them and yet seeing them rise again and take their place on the line . . . that it changed me.

What did that fireman say that night on Nob Hill? That it surprised him when people took advantage of disaster. I feel such a deep shame when I remember that. Because that is what I'm doing. Taking advantage of disaster and taking advantage of poor Lily Sump.

I am going to tell the truth to Mr. Crandall when I see him. Just knowing that makes me feel better. I will tell him about the ledger and ask him to restore my family's fortunes and just hope that he will do the right thing. Maybe the disaster has changed him, too.

The Jennardis have set up a feeding station. They had loaded up a wagon with everything they could from their grocery, knowing that food would be needed. For hours today we stood and handed out what food they had. Cheese, sausage, olives, tinned sardines.

I asked Jake if the store had burned, and he said he didn't know. Certainly the rest of the foodstuffs they had to leave have spoiled. "No telling what we'll find or what we'll be able to salvage. Have to wait until things cool off to check the safe. Could have lost everything," he said, but his tone was cheerful. "Pop says starting from scratch isn't so bad if you have enough friends." He said *friends* with extra meaning and for the first time since I left Philadelphia I felt at home in the world.

I just realized while writing this that the weather has changed. It is chilly, the mildness of the air gone. And I realize that the sky above me is not full of smoke, but clouds.

I feel something on my face, my hands. I jump away, afraid of cinders.

Then I realize what it is, and I lift my face to the sky, to the blessing that is falling on us.

Rain.

LATER
11 P.M.

The rain will put out whatever embers are left. The city is safe.

I am not.

I forgot of course how much could go wrong so quickly.

I was slicing oranges for the children in Mission Park when I saw Mr. Crandall walking toward me.

"Lily!"

My mouth went dry as fear pumped through me. Jake was standing right next to me, helping his mother to chop the stale bread, which will be toasted and then thrown into the vegetable soup.

Mr. Crandall said he'd been looking everywhere for me, and he looked truly exhausted. I told him I was sorry, and that I was planning to go to him when I finished with the food line (and here he looked at the line and back at me, as if to say, *Lily Sump is feeding refugees?*)

Jake turned to me with his easy smile. "So. I finally discover your name. Lily."

"I—"

Mr. Crandall took notice of Jake in his shabby working clothes, his grimy cap.

He nodded politely.

"Thank you for looking after Miss Sump."

"Miss *Sump*?"

Oh, Jake, I prayed, *please don't give me away.* I could see it in his face, how he knew that I couldn't be a fine lady, he had met me in a kitchen with my hands full of carrots.

"I'm sure we're very grateful." Mr. Crandall fished in his pocket and held out a coin. Jake just looked at it. Then he looked at me.

"This is Mr. Crandall," I said. "My father's attorney."

"Your father . . ."

"My father and mother were killed in the quake," I said. "And our maid, Minnie Bonner. Mr. Crandall found me that morning and has taken care of me ever since. Otherwise I don't know what would have happened to me. I am alone." I emphasized that last word, *alone,* hoping he would sympathize in even one small way.

"Minnie Bonner." Jake repeated the name. "The maid, you say." I saw that he didn't quite understand, but something happened behind his eyes, and I knew I was no longer his friend.

He took a step back. He stuck his hands in his pockets, refusing the coin. "No, thank you, sir," he said. "The Jennardis don't believe in profiting from disaster."

The words sliced me to ribbons. How I wished I could explain! But within a moment Mr. Crandall had taken my arm and led me away.

Now I am in Mrs. Crandall's sister's house, a pretty cottage with a view of an enormous hill with two identical crests. It is called Twin Peaks. When the fog rolls in, it spills around the two crests, leaving Mrs. Flynn's neighborhood bathed in bright sunshine.

I've been given the nicest guest room, which makes me ashamed, because of course I only got it because I was Lily Sump. Mrs. Crandall's sister — Mrs. Flynn — is very kind. She gave me a salve for my blistered palms and wrapped my hands in bandages.

She is sharper than Mrs. Crandall, however. Earlier we were sitting in the parlor and she was going over what was in the larder — food is scarce — and lamenting that she only had a few eggs left and no hope of getting more. What could she do with only three eggs? I suggested she whip the eggs into a mayonnaise and stir it into the fish soup. I asked her if she had garlic. Papa had taught me this trick.

She stopped what she was doing and gave me a quick surprised glance, for what rich man's daughter knows how to make a garlic mayonnaise?

I said I used to slip downstairs to the kitchen and talk to the cook in Philadelphia.

"I see," she murmured.

I then spoiled my explanation by rising in order to clear the table. I sat down quickly with a thump. I don't think she noticed.

It is not easy to remember that I am a rich girl who never spent time in a tavern kitchen, never cleared a table.

The sisters are polite to each other, but it's rather like the past three days — dynamite could go off at any moment.

Tomorrow I am going to tell Mr. Crandall the truth.

APRIL 22, 1906
SUNDAY
4 P.M.

Oh, diary, I am trapped worse than before.

This afternoon Mr. Crandall called me into the study. He had skipped church in order to walk to Russian Hill to check on his house. It is still standing—the neighbors who remained were able to save his, as it stood in the middle of the ones they were saving. Mrs. Crandall is already making plans to return.

He asked if I had something to tell him. I felt my heart start to beat so quickly. My face flushed. He saw my discomfort and sighed.

Then he told me that upon inspecting his house he met a young man who was searching for me. Could I guess who that was? I said no, my heart still threatening to leap out of my chest.

"Your fiancé," he said.

My face registered my shock, but luckily he thought I was only surprised at being caught out.

"You might have told me," he said.

I couldn't speak, which he took for embarrassment. I was remembering Lily's face in the moments right before the world exploded. *I am running* to *something,* she had said. Now I know what she was planning. Not to run away, but to run away with someone and get married.

She was in love. That was the light I saw in her eyes.

"He has been searching the city for you," he said. "He was quite overcome to hear that you are, indeed, alive. He had been at the house and saw that it had been burned to the ground." Then he hesitated. "I am not your father, Lily. Yet I am here to protect you, to stand in for your father. This young man is not suitable for you."

He drummed his fingers on the desk and began his lecture while I wondered, *Who is Lily's sweetheart? Who could it be?* And suddenly such sadness washed over me. I thought of her happy face, ready to start her life. It wasn't fair that at her happiest moment the walls came crashing down.

And what of this man, her fiancé? Panic and shame hit me with the force of a slap. Mr. Crandall had no doubt told him that Lily was alive. He had despaired, and then he had been handed his happiness, and now I would have to tell him that she was dead. He would lose her twice. I would have to deliver that unimaginable pain.

I had stopped listening, but then I heard Mr. Crandall say this:

"In short, Mr. Jewell is not a gentleman."

And my mind stopped short and turned around.

Andrew Jewell? And *Lily*?

And suddenly I remembered Lily on the train, always taking that walk while her mother napped, and that glimpse I saw of her, standing with a tall, slim man, their backs to me. . . .

But he'd seen us on the street just a few days before. He'd heard Mr. Crandall call me Lily.

Or perhaps I was mistaken. I must have been mistaken. Or else why was he here?

My mind whirled. Could Andrew Jewell have loved Lily?

"And I must urge you to dissolve the engagement."

"Perhaps you're right," I said. "It was a mistake."

It was almost comical, Mr. Crandall's look of surprise. His mouth dropped open. It was clear he hadn't expected his lecture to work quite so efficiently.

"I'm happy to hear you've come to your senses," Mr. Crandall said.

"I will write to him," I said.

"That would be difficult, as he has no home, along with half of San Francisco," Mr. Crandall pointed out. "In any event, he is waiting in the parlor."

I had to break off just now as there was a knock on the door. Mrs. Flynn has brought me a cup of tea. As she changed the dressings on my hands, she said gently that I could stay as long as I liked in her house.

I couldn't meet her eyes.

"You don't know me," I said.

She turned over my hands very gently so that my red, blistered palms showed. "I know enough," she said.

Now I've wrapped a borrowed shawl around

myself. My whole body is shaking as I contemplate what I am facing, what I have to do.

But let me go back to when I walked into the parlor to see Andrew Jewell.

It took every bit of courage I possessed to walk through that door. I didn't know what I would find, an anxious fiancé overjoyed at seeing his beloved . . . and then crushed by the new information that she had perished. Or would I find someone who had guessed my deception?

I wasn't sure what would be worse.

He was standing by the window when I slipped inside and closed the door after me. I didn't say anything for a long moment as he turned. We stood facing each other and then, slowly, he smiled.

"So, Jock Bonner's daughter," he said. "Do you want to tell me what scheme you've been working?"

I hesitated, not knowing what to say or where to start.

"Come, come now. Shyness doesn't become you. What happened to Lily, first of all?"

"I am sorry to tell you this, Mr. Jewell, but your

fiancée was killed instantly the morning of the quake. I realize now that she was on her way to see you."

"Yes. I had persuaded her on the train journey to run away together."

"You must be experiencing great grief right now."

"Terrible grief," he said. "I am on my knees."

"Yes, I can see how much the news has affected you."

He didn't miss the scorn in my voice. "Poor Lily," he said. "Such an unhappy girl. So ready to have someone to depend on. I would have *tried* to make her happy. It was not to be."

"So you really meant to marry her?"

"That was the plan."

"But Mr. Sump would have disinherited her."

"I had some reasons to convince him not to oppose his daughter's choice."

"You mean you would have blackmailed him."

He smiled. "Such an ugly word for persuasion."

I sat down, shocked at the depths of this man's

cruelty. Poor Lily. He hadn't loved her at all.

"Now," he said. "Tell me what happened, and how you have managed to fool Mr. Crandall."

I told him how Mr. Crandall had found me and at first just assumed I was Lily, and that I didn't correct him. That I wanted him to agree to give the tavern back to my parents since Mr. Sump had cheated them out of it. He could make things right.

He just laughed. "You little fool, Crandall is as crooked as Sump," he said. "Now he gets to handle all the money. I can imagine how that thrills him. He wants to *be* Sump. Now he can be. He'll never agree. Unless . . ."

I watched the calculation in his face. He studied me closely for a moment. "So Lily is dead, and you are alive, and now you are an heiress to the Sump millions. You're quite the gambler for a young lady."

I deserved that, but I didn't like hearing it. "And you are a two-bit thief who would take advantage of a sweet, trusting girl like Lily," I said.

"Hardly two bits, petal. And Lily was . . . not so sweet. She wanted an escape, and I provided one. Is what I was going to do much worse than what you did, Miss Bonner?"

"I had a reason."

"Oh, we all have *reasons*."

His smile made me feel cold. Fear coiled inside me. I realized that I had no idea how far this man would go to get back what had almost been in his grasp.

"I'm going to tell Mr. Crandall the truth," I said, starting toward the door. "This has gone far enough."

He grabbed my arm. "Oh, no, you aren't, petal," he said. "We're in this together now."

"No," I said. "I'm not like you. I know of your association with Mr. Sump. I know he paid you and I know how much. I know that you were involved in the scheme to cheat my father out of our tavern."

"What a suspicious little mind you have. I'm impressed."

"I don't have mere suspicions. I have proof!"

There is where I made my error, diary. I spoke without thinking because I was so afraid and angry.

He cocked his head and narrowed his gaze. "You have proof, you say? How? Where?"

I didn't answer, and he took my hand and squeezed it. The burns I had sustained from Friday screamed in protest, and I let out a gasp of pain. He merely asked me *where* again. And squeezed.

"A ledger!" I gasped. I fell back on the sofa as he released me.

"Of course that old miser had to write everything down. Well, that makes things more interesting, doesn't it? Where is this ledger?"

I told him I had buried it in a fireproof box.

He paced around the room. Despite the pain in my hand, I felt a kind of numbness. I couldn't think of what to do or how to stop this. It was as though a spool of thread had fallen from my lap and was now busily unraveling itself as it rolled away across the floor.

"This was a brilliant stroke, Miss Bonner! We have him now. The question is, how best to work the scheme. . . ."

He told me his plan. We follow through on the engagement. We marry quickly. No one will find it odd — it's what people do after disasters, seek a new life, he said.

"Once you marry, you can control Sump's money," he said.

"You mean you will control it," I said.

"We will seek an equitable disbursement," he said. "Don't worry, we will share in our good fortune. After a suitable period, I will run off. Poor Lily Sump, deserted by her no-good husband. You will go on with your life, with or without Sump's money, that's none of my concern. My guess is that you will get quite used to feeling comfortable in silks and satins, and will remain Lily Sump. Unless some long-lost relative shows up, that's always a danger. But that's your dilemma."

He told me not to be so shocked, that he had to make his way in the world just like any man, and did I think Mr. Sump was anything less than a crook himself?

I told him there was a flaw in his plan. Mr.

Crandall was my guardian and he would never agree to the marriage.

"You let me handle him," he said. "Remember, we have the ledger."

I didn't like the way he said *we*, diary.

In a match such as this, the one who is afraid, who shows that fear — loses. He could see how afraid I was. He knew he had me cornered.

He told me I had no choice. It was either this, or jail. He would have no compunction, he assured me, turning me in to the police. He would play the grieving fiancé. Sympathy would be on his side — how terrible it was, he said mockingly, to walk the charred streets of San Francisco looking for his love, find out she was alive, and then have his hopes dashed! I would be thrown into a cell and no doubt Mr. Crandall would turn the key.

"Do you know what they would do to you?" he said. "To someone who would take the identity of a poor dead girl?"

"I can't go to jail, I'm only fourteen," I said.

"Really? Such a prodigy! What impressive

criminal skills you have at such a young age. Don't worry, there are worse places than jail for criminal children."

There was a knock at the door. "Is everything all right?" Mr. Crandall asked through the door.

Jewell grabbed my bandaged hand and pulled me to my feet.

"Let us tell him the happy news," he hissed in my ear.

I have to keep stopping and walking around the room. I feel as though I can't breathe. As though the smoke rising from the ruins is inside my lungs. I cradle my hand against my chest. It feels hot and painful.

Mr. Crandall coolly informed Jewell that I was under his guardianship and could not marry without his permission until the age of twenty-one. As I was only sixteen — or, at least, that's what Mr. Crandall thought — Mr. Jewell would have to wait five years.

"And mark my words, you will wait every second of it," he said.

Jewell played his part to the end. He said in a revoltingly steady voice that he would wait every one of those seconds in order to achieve the dream of union with his beloved.

Mr. Crandall snorted.

"I know who and what you are, Mr. Jewell," he said. "And if you think I would allow my client's daughter to marry you, you are mistaken."

"Say what you wish, Mr. Crandall." He turned, his next words to me. "I am not giving up."

As I saw him to the front door, he said in my ear, "I will come for you, and we will dig up that book."

APRIL 23, 1906
MONDAY
3 A.M.

I will leave and he will never find me.

But where will I go?

4 A.M.

Jake's eyes are haunting me.

5 A.M.

If only I could go back and change everything. Everything.

How can I extricate myself from this web I have woven?

3 P.M.

We have returned to Russian Hill. Mr. Crandall got his automobile back, much the worse for wear, but still running.

We said good-bye to Mrs. Flynn and it was obvious that this would not mark a new beginning for the two families. Mrs. Crandall made it clear that she did not approve of her sister's choice in husbands or appreciate her pretty, modest house. She had bigger ambitions. It was also clear that Mrs. Flynn bid us good-bye with relief.

Yet she saw my trouble in my eyes and took me aside to say that if I ever needed help, she could be someone to call on.

Now I know what my father means about "honest eyes." I think of Mrs. Flynn, and I think of Jake, and all I want to do is confess and make things right.

As we drove through the city, we saw from the comfort of an automobile the wreckage and destruction. There were streets we passed without a house standing. Sometimes there would be a flight of stone steps leading nowhere. The ruins still smoked despite the rain. There was a sweetish smoky smell to the air, unpleasant and sick-making.

Hundreds, thousands, have lost their homes and now live in tents. Who can count how many lives have been lost?

No one in this city has escaped. Even if they still have a roof over their heads.

Even though the smell of death and fire was everywhere, I didn't see despair. I saw families camping outside on their lawns. Stoves set up on sidewalks. Children running through the streets. A man playing a cheerful tune on a piano dragged onto a blackened lawn.

I am sure that we also passed those who will

try to profit by this calamity, who looted, who were cowards, who did not help their neighbor but only themselves.

Do I want to be among their number?

The hours I spent fighting the fire were the hardest I've ever worked. The exhaustion was overwhelming and yet we kept going, bringing water, slapping out sparks with carpets and brooms and sometimes even our hands. I have the burns to prove it.

I wish I could get back to how I felt that day. That I had a purpose that was real and fine.

When we crossed Van Ness, one side remained with its grand houses and the other side was just dirt and crumbling walls and charred wood. We drove past and here on the east side we saw just bare hills. The houses that remained stood out like broken teeth. Mr. Crandall just stopped the car for a moment while we took it in. Then we climbed the hill and around us was just . . . nothing, collapsed walls and a pile of bricks here or there. The great emptiness we saw was inside each of us. Even Mrs. Crandall stopped talking.

Every house was gone on Sacramento Street. The only thing left of the Sump mansion was the blackened and twisted gate. On the crown of Nob Hill, only the Flood mansion survived on California, and that because it was built of stone. The interior was burned out. The gleaming white marble of the new Fairmont Hotel was blackened with soot.

It is all gone. The buildings downtown that survived are black with smoke and mere shells.

We knew this had happened, but seeing it took the breath from us.

Mr. Crandall slowly drove up Russian Hill to Green Street. When he pulled up in front of the house Mrs. Crandall burst into tears.

The house inside is full of broken pottery and overturned chairs and the walls are blackened, but the Crandalls are better off than most and I hope they know it.

APRIL 24, 1906
TUESDAY

At lunch I was pushing around my food on my plate when Mr. Crandall came in late and took his seat at the table, apologizing to us and shaking his head.

"This is an extraordinary disaster, I must say," he said, picking up his fork. "I can't get cash from my bank or milk delivered or cook a meal inside my house, and yet somehow I find a deliveryman has located me and is delivering a large crate to our front yard."

Mrs. Crandall hurried to the window. I craned my neck and could see from my seat the enormous wooden crate lying on the lawn.

"Apparently the man is one of those souls who knows his duty and is determined to fulfill it no matter if the world has crashed down upon his ears. He drove the crate over from Alameda, where it has been sitting since the earthquake. I wonder he doesn't have anything better to do, but I expect he came so that I would pay him."

Mrs. Crandall asked what was in the crate.

"It was sent from Philadelphia—a painting that was going to hang in the study of the mansion. I'm sure you know it, Lily."

Mrs. Crandall patted my hand and said

something about how lovely it was that at least I will have familiar things around me.

"Much too large for our house, I'm afraid. I don't know quite what to do with it, but we do want to get it indoors. We'll have to uncrate it soon."

"This just proves that we need a bigger house," Mrs. Crandall said. "Lily should live in the style she is accustomed to."

"I find it unseemly to speak of building a larger house when so many have none," Mr. Crandall said. But his gaze turned thoughtful. "Still, you are right, my dear. It is never too soon to start planning. There will be those needing cash for parcels they own and will be willing to sell. . . ."

"I do not think it wrong to plan for the future," Mrs. Crandall said. "San Francisco must be rebuilt, and quickly. Why shouldn't we plan? I'm only thinking of Lily. We need to provide her with what dear Mr. and Mrs. Sump would want. We could rebuild on the same site. Lily would have her home back. Something more to our taste, of course."

A glance traveled between them. Mr. Crandall smoothed his mustache and smiled. "Yes," he said. "We must think of Lily."

I stand now at my bedroom window, looking down.

The painting Mrs. Sump spoke of back in Philadelphia. The painting she had posed for. With Lily.

When Mr. Crandall uncrates it, he will see an image of a girl of my size and shape. But she will not be me.

I am close to panic now, but I can also feel something pulsing underneath my fear: relief.

I don't know what will happen to me or where I should go or how I should get there, but I think I must run away. The question is, where to?

APRIL 25, 1906
WEDNESDAY

Diary, you are not going to believe what happened. It seemed a miracle.

This morning we were out of food and there is no more in the stores, which are all burned out anyway. There are plenty of provisions in the parks and squares, so I offered to wait in the line for whatever they are giving away. Mrs. Crandall gratefully accepted. Her cook and maid still have not returned, and she hates doing the housework and waiting in the lines for food and water.

It is a long way to carry provisions from Golden Gate Park but there is a provision line set up in Jefferson Square, which is closer. I waited in the line for two hours. I didn't mind. It was a fine day and there is so much to look at. I was able to think about my own dilemma but also see other people in worse shape than I was.

My plan was to try to get to Golden Gate Park before dark, where I could lose myself among the refugees. Until then I must act as normal as possible. When Mr. Crandall unpacks the painting he will know why I left. He will be gone most of the day, in meetings with the committees being set up for the rebuilding of the city, and he told

Mrs. Crandall that he will not be home for supper. Still, he could uncrate the painting tonight
or tomorrow.

As I turned away with my basket I saw a tall
man standing still in the middle of the square,
scanning the crowd. My heart stopped.

He must have sensed me more than saw me,
standing stock-still while people swirled around
me, because he swiveled and his gaze met mine.

Papa.

"Minnie!"

I heard my name on his lips, my very own
name, and it was like sweet honey to hear it.

We ran to each other and he swept me up in his
arms. He smelled like smoke and his hands were
grimy and I could see soot in the lines around his
eyes. He was the best sight I have ever seen.

He held me against him, murmuring over and
over, "My girl, my girl." When I pulled away his
eyes were full of tears. "I thought you were . . . I
heard . . ."

And then I had to wait while he composed

himself. I saw the great love he had for me. I'll never doubt it again.

"I heard the maid had been killed," he said. A sob escaped him. "I didn't believe it, I *couldn't*—"

"But why are you here?" I asked him. It seemed such a miracle. I thought I had run out of surprises.

We sat on the grass and he told me everything. He had been one day behind me—he arrived the day after the quake. Back in Philadelphia he tried to find me and Mama, but she left no forwarding address. Finally he got the address of her rooming house from friends. She gave him Andrew Jewell's card—actually, she threw it at him.

How many times, he said to me, *can one woman forgive?* She said she was out of forgiveness.

So he tracked down Andrew Jewell and discovered that he'd departed for California, leaving a substantial hotel bill. Associates were also looking for him. They called him "Slippery Andy." This supposedly wealthy young businessman was a gambler, a cardsharp. *A common criminal!* Papa said, shaking his head.

"I should have known," he said. "I've seen enough of his type in my time."

He knew then that he'd been cheated in that game. "Maybe I deserved it for playing at all, Min," he said. "So I decided to use my last monies to buy a railroad ticket. I figured I could get a job out here, keep an eye on you, and try to find Jewell. Instead I arrived the day after the quake and had quite a time trying to get into San Francisco to find you. I was able to send your mother a telegram from Oakland, telling her I was looking."

He has been looking for me for almost a week. When he saw the Sump mansion burned and heard a maid died, he almost lost hope. But he didn't stop looking.

"Thank the Lord I didn't tell your mother what I learned," he said. "We must get a letter to her first thing. I heard they have the mail running now, and you don't even need a stamp. She must be frantic with worry for you. And we'll find a way to get you a train ticket. . . ."

I started to cry and could not stop. I sobbed

and sobbed until the ash on his coat mixed with my tears and we were covered in a gray film.

"I can't go back. . . . I can't face her. . . ."

"But why not, *ma petite*?"

"Because I can't face her eyes."

And then I told him everything.

He dropped his head in his hands during the telling, and I couldn't see his expression. I was afraid of what he would say. He didn't speak for a long time. He kept his hand over his eyes, his mouth a line.

I thought he was angry at me, but I saw tears slip through his fingers.

"Look what I have done to you," he said. "Forgive me."

Diary, I love my father. I forgive him. But I do not trust him.

I told him about the ledger, and the cash, and the bonds. What if it's too much temptation for him?

Did I get myself in a worse hole?

I have to fix this.

I think I have a plan. But first, here is what happened next.

We left the food and water with a family my father had come to trust, who were staying in Jefferson Square. Then we set out for Golden Gate Park. I knew Andrew Jewell was staying there.

The tents are set up in rows that stretch as far as the eye can see. It is all very orderly. Thousands of people here, so how can we find him?

My father stood, scanning the tents. "Not a problem, *chérie*. Where there are this many men, there will be a game. We just need to ask a few likely suspects."

We found him near the Japanese gardens, in the middle of a poker game at a table drawn up near a cypress tree. Some of the men looked as though they had been playing all night. Papa just stood and waited until Mr. Jewell looked up and saw him. He looked surprised but covered it up quickly.

"Well, if it isn't the Frenchman. Can I deal you

in, Jock? Fellas, this is Jock from Philly, a good man and an able player."

"No more playing for me, Slippery Andy," Papa said.

The men at the table eyed Jewell a little nervously now that they heard his nickname.

"I think I'll fold," Jewell said.

He rose from the table and followed my father a few paces away.

"What are you doing here, Jock?" he asked.

"Came looking for my daughter."

"Lucky you found her. Lots of people missing."

"Found her, yes, and in better circumstances than I left her."

"So . . . you know."

"I know there's an attorney who thinks she's Lily Sump. It's a good scheme, and I hear you're looking for a piece of it."

"Well, I thought I'd step in. Little girl like that can't work a con this big by herself."

My father clapped him on the back. "Ah, you're a good man, Jewell, to look out for my little girl." He squeezed his shoulder.

Something heavy passed between them, some kind of exchange that had menace in it.

"What are you thinking, then?" Jewell asked my father.

"I'm thinking a two-thirds split. Seeing that you owe me a tavern."

I could see the calculation in Jewell's eyes as he looked from Papa to me.

"I don't owe you anything, Bonner, but I guess you've a right to see to your own interests, and your daughter's. Plenty to go around."

"Good, because there's a change in plans. Crandall is on the verge of discovering that she's not Lily Sump after all. It appears that a painting has been delivered and he's planning on uncrating it tonight or tomorrow. So we haven't much time."

"There's a ledger—"

"If you think he'll give in because of some book full of numbers, you're not as sharp as I thought you were, Andy," my father said. "Sure, there could be an investigation, but how far will it get when the mayor himself is corrupt? Crandall will whistle up a chorus of 'I Don't Care' right in your face. But if you're smart and come with me, we can all share in the bounty, thanks to my little girl here."

"I'm listening."

"She buried a strongbox outside the mansion. She told me what's in it. Cash. Lots of it. And she described what sounded to me like bearer bonds. Who cares about the ledger when there's a possible million in that box? You know men like Sump always have walking-away money. Well, this is it."

Jewell's eyes gleamed. "You sure?"

"I'm sure. You in?"

"I'm in."

So we made a plan. We meet at the site of the burned Sump house at 4 A.M. That's the empty hour, Papa said—when the early risers are still in bed, and those who stay out late are already home.

I retrieved the water and food and brought it back to Mrs. Crandall. We ate a quick supper and now I'm in my room with the light out. Mr Crandall has not returned. As soon as Mrs. Crandall retires I will sneak out to meet my father.

APRIL 26, 1906
THURSDAY

I'm thinking this will be my last entry. Once I record what happened, I am going to put this book away and not look at it for fifty years.

We had to be careful because of the sentries. We slid from shadow to shadow until we got near the top of Nob Hill. We turned down Sacramento and walked through the twisted and broken wrought-iron gates. Andrew Jewell was waiting there.

I found the three stacked bricks, charred black. I nudged the dirt with my toe. "Here."

We had not considered that the shovel I had used would be useless, twisted metal with no handle. We had to dig with stones, and the bent metal of the shovel, and then our hands. Lucky for us I had not buried the box too deep.

Jewell reached in for it eagerly, then let out a hiss. "It's still hot."

My father covered his hands with his sleeves and lifted it out. The lock was still intact. I had the key in my pocket, the watch ornament. I handed it to my father.

"No," Jewell said. "Let me."

I handed him the key.

He slid the key into the lock and opened the box.

He drew in a breath at the sight of the neatly stacked cash.

It happened so fast we didn't have time to blink. I saw a faint orange line, and the next thing I knew the contents were ablaze.

With a howl, Jewell reached in and tried to take out the cash but it was burning paper now, and he threw it down.

"You tricked me!" he screamed. "You set it on fire!"

"No trick," my father said. He stared down at the still-burning contents. With his boot, he flipped over the box and quickly kicked dirt over the ledger, putting out the fire. "I'm guessing it was just too hot to open. When the oxygen hit, it ignited. We should have waited, maybe."

"*Maybe?*" Jewell screamed. "Are you really

standing there watching a million dollars go up in smoke, calm as you please?"

"I don't see how shouting is going to bring it back. Though it might bring the sentries and we hardly want that," Papa pointed out.

Jewell stamped away. He stood a few feet from us, his shoulders heaving.

"You knew," Papa whispered.

I shrugged my shoulders.

Papa shook his head, and then he laughed.

"Now you're *laughing*?" Jewell said, turning around furiously.

"I don't see anything better to do. Sometimes things work, sometimes they don't."

"This isn't over, Jock Bonner," Jewell said. He brushed past us and disappeared into the gloom.

We heard his footsteps echo for a while, and then there was only silence and stars.

"Oh, it's over," my father said softly. "He is a man of empty threats."

"Were you going to take the money?" I asked.

"He wouldn't have given us the chance. Jewell

had a gun in his pocket. He was planning to take everything—but he would have left the ledger."

"You mean you wouldn't have fought him for it? It was a fortune!"

"It was a considerable temptation," he said. "But not worth it, I think."

I don't know if he was telling the truth. But I've decided to believe it.

Without speaking, we climbed one more block to the crown of Nob Hill. We walked past the broken stone lions of one of the mansions to the only thing that remained of the Towne mansion, the steps leading to the marble-columned portico. We climbed the steps, my father and I, and gazed out. By the light of the pale moon we could see the skeletal dome of City Hall through the empty frame of the columns.

There were scattered lights around the hills, from outdoor stoves, I guess. That was the only way I knew there were people out there, tucked into these bare hills where once there had been houses and restaurants and stores.

I had a strange sensation right then, diary. As

though I were on the top of a world about to be born. I could smell the bay, the wild salt smell of it. For the first time in a week, it overpowered the smell of decay.

"Heard lots of hammering and sawing today," Papa said. "People starting to rebuild already."

"You'd think they'd all be leaving," I said. "Scared to live here after what happened. But they're staying."

"That's what faith is," he said.

We stared out at the graying sky, the flares of light.

"Plus, it's a kind of paradise here, isn't it?" he asked.

"If you don't mind the earth cracking open," I said.

"Everything has a flaw, Min. Even cities. Doesn't spoil the beauty one bit."

That first day I arrived—I thought of it then. The blue bay and the white houses and the sky, and the air so fresh at the top of the hill. How exhilarating it all was.

"This is our chance to start over," he said. "We could make something new."

"But how? We have nothing."

"We have this." He showed me the ledger in his hand, charred and black.

"But it's ruined."

"Crandall won't know that. He doesn't need to see inside it; he just needs to see it exists."

"And what will we ask for in return? The tavern?"

"We could. Or we could ask for the money from the sale."

"But why would he say yes, after what I've done?"

"Because of what you saw in this book. And I do not think a man with so much to lose will pursue this any further. He has too much to gain."

"And then . . ."

He made a suggestion that surprised me. "What if we wrote to your mother and asked her to come out here? Perhaps we are holding on to something we don't want anymore. We're just in the habit of thinking it's our only hope. The tavern will be gone soon anyway, *chérie*. The city is changing and leaving us behind. But we could start something here. This strikes me as a place people may start over again."

"Do you think she'll say yes?"

"If she doesn't, we'll go back. We'll be together. Whether she lets me in the door or not. I don't know what will happen. I just know I have a way to make amends. Thanks to you, Min."

I don't know what will happen, either. But when everything is gone, what can you do but have faith?

We could see the beginnings of sunrise now, just a glow of pink in the sky. We walked back down the hill in that ravishing light. Outside the house on Green Street we saw the remains of the crate neatly stacked on the lawn, ready to be taken away.

I stopped on the stairs and looked through the window. The painting leaned against the wall. Lily's gaze stared out at me, her mother's heavy hand on her shoulder. She looked nothing like me at all.

At the dining room table I saw Mr. Crandall smoking a cigar, sitting and waiting for me.

You can have your life back now, Lily. I won't be living it. Rest in peace.

Papa took my hand. "Ready?"

I'm ready.

EPILOGUE

When Minnie admitted her deception, Mr. Crandall's fury blasted her eardrums. Mrs. Crandall threatened to telephone the police. Then she realized that she didn't have telephone service.

Mr. Crandall calmed down when Jock Bonner produced the ledger and suggested that it would be to all of their benefits to let the deception be passed along to earthquake shock and upset. He offered to toss the ledger into the stove outside, let it burn, and start over. He also pointed out that without Lily, Mr. Crandall now had full power over the Sump estate.

Mr. and Mrs. Crandall calmed down quickly.

Mr. Crandall paid the Bonners for the sale of the tavern. Minnie and her father had an anxious ten days of waiting before hearing from her mother. She informed them that she would come to San Francisco, but she had not forgiven her husband.

With the money from the tavern sale the Bonners built and furnished a restaurant in downtown San Francisco that they called Lily's. Mrs. Bonner didn't talk to her husband for thirty-two days, which was surely a record. Lily's became a favorite restaurant during the rebuilding of downtown, and the customers stayed loyal — politicians, journalists, businessmen, and writers.

Hugh Crandall went on to establish the Sump Trust, which he administered. The Sump Trust was an important financial partner in the rebuilding of San Francisco. Mr. Crandall became a rich and successful attorney specializing in commercial real estate. He and his wife built a showplace on Nob Hill on the site of the old Sump mansion.

Minnie never forgot the Jennardis. They reopened their grocery in six months, in a new building in North Beach, the Italian section of San Francisco. Minnie often thought about seeking out Jake to explain what had happened to her and her family, but she could not get up the nerve. Then, nine years later, at the Panama-Pacific International Exposition of 1915, they ran into each other. Although so much time had passed, they knew each other instantly. Within a year they were married and moved into a small house on Telegraph Hill with a view of the bay.

Jake Jennardi became a partner in the restaurant, and it became a San Francisco institution, popular with locals and tourists, and known for its French and Italian food. Today it is run by their great-great-granddaughter, Alessandra Jennardi.

Minnie and Jake had three children. Their eldest son, Dante, took over the restaurant when they decided to take early retirement and divide their time between the city and their house on a vineyard in Napa Valley. Jake died in his sleep at the age of eighty-three, and Minnie lived until she was ninety-one. For the last ten years of her life, Minnie was an honored guest at the April 18 earthquake anniversary ceremony at Twentieth and Church Streets, when the hydrant there was repainted gold in memory of its role in saving the Mission District and Noe Valley from the fire.

Jock Bonner would still take off for weeks at a time, but he never gambled again. He was a beloved grandfather to Minnie's children for a few short years. He died of a heart attack at the age of fifty-five, while sailing with a friend on San Francisco Bay.

Hazel Bonner surprised the family by marrying again, and lived a long life with her second husband, a professor of geology.

Mr. Crandall and his wife had two daughters. When her father died, his daughter Lavinia took over the trust in partnership with her cousin and best friend, Delia Flynn. Together they expanded its interests from commercial buildings into the nonprofit world of libraries and museums. The Sump Trust funded many projects in Chinatown and working-class neighborhoods, starting libraries and school lunch programs during the Depression. Lavinia never got along with her mother.

Andrew "Slippery Andy" Jewell started a new life in Los Angeles. He worked in vaudeville doing card and magic tricks and then as an extra in the developing silent film industry. He was shot during a poker game in 1922 at the age of forty-two.

LIFE IN AMERICA
IN 1906

HISTORICAL NOTE

"There is no water, and still less soap.
We have no city, but lots of hope."
—*Anonymous inscription scribbled
on the ruins of Market Street*

At 5:12 on the morning of April 18, 1906, a powerful earthquake ripped through San Francisco at an estimated 7,000 miles per hour, throwing many people out of their beds. Some never made it that far—95 percent of all the chimneys in the city collapsed in that shock, some of them on people still asleep.

Those who were awake and outside reported that sidewalks rolled like rough ocean waves, and deep cracks appeared in the street only to close up again. Some buildings fell in a thundering crash, and others remained intact but were knocked off their foundations, tilting crazily over the street.

The Valencia Hotel collapsed like an accordion, and those on the fourth story stepped over the debris and walked straight out into the street. Those in the lower floors were not so lucky. An estimated one hundred people lost their lives in that hotel, some in the initial collapse, some drowning as the water mains burst and flooded the layers beneath the street.

There was no system of measurement for earthquakes in 1906, but today's geologists estimate the quake at anywhere between 7.9 and 8.2 on the Richter scale: a catastrophic event.

Those who survived the shock had no way to know that the worst was yet to come. Together, the quake and ensuing three-day firestorm were one of the worst natural disasters in United States history. More than fifty fires began in the first hours after the quake, some growing to join others until there was a solid wall of flame a mile and a half long.

Volcanoes smoke and storms build, but earthquakes give no warning. The day before the earthquake was fair and sunny, the first day of delightful weather after a damp and chilly spring.

If a city can have a collective mood, San Francisco was in a cheerful frame of mind. The world-famous tenor Enrico Caruso was in town, and all of society turned out to see his performance in the opera *Carmen*. San Franciscans were proud of their city, the biggest and most important metropolis west of Chicago. With a population of about four hundred thousand, it was the nation's ninth-largest city. It was a busy port, the gateway to Asia and the Pacific, and a center for business and manufacturing. It had the largest population of Chinese in any American city — estimated at 14,000 in 1905 — most of them living in the densely populated blocks of Chinatown.

The completion of the transcontinental railroad in 1869 had brought fortunes not only to the men who built the railroads — the owners of those mansions on top of Nob Hill known as the Big Four: Leland Stanford, Collis Huntington, Mark Hopkins, and Charles Crocker — but others who profited from the continuing expansion of the rails and the explosion in population.

Travel on the railroads became easier and

more comfortable with the innovations of George Pullman, inventor of the Pullman sleeper car. More and more people began to consider a trip to California something they could do, and once they arrived they could stay in hotels such as the Palace, which promised luxury and refinement. A trip out West was no longer considered dangerous and uncomfortable, but a relatively easy week-long journey that even the most apprehensive Easterner could contemplate.

In 1906, business was booming, the rich were getting richer, and new inventions promised to make life more pleasant even for the poor. Most of the major advances in technology of the twentieth century had already been invented: the automobile, the telephone, the airplane, moving pictures, the electric light, the phonograph. These marvels would, over the years, be streamlined, improved, made easier to operate or more pleasing to look at — but they already existed in 1906, and there was a general feeling that they would soon be a part of everyday life, and the world was changing for the better.

With change and growth came opportunity, especially for the rich men who ran things. The government of San Francisco operated on a system of bribes and payoffs, thanks to a corrupt city council and a mayor, Eugene Schmitz, who was controlled by the political boss Abe Ruef. There were systems to be built and expanded—the pipes, rails, wires, and cables that would bring water, electricity, telephones, and public transportation to the people of San Francisco. All required permits and contracts, and politicians were happy to do favors for the right amount of cash. The situation in San Francisco had grown so corrupt that the reform effort reached all the way to the White House and President Theodore Roosevelt. After the quake, a federal investigation into graft and corruption continued, and political boss Abe Ruef was convicted and jailed. Mayor Schmitz was also convicted, but his sentence was overturned. The mayor had been hailed as a decisive leader during the crisis, and did rise to the occasion, so many San Franciscans did not want to see him imprisoned.

A city of wooden houses, narrow streets, steep hills, and gusty winds, San Francisco was especially vulnerable to fire. The reservoirs that fed water to the city used wooden trestles for their pipelines, often crisscrossing over the San Andreas Fault, which was known as the Tomales-Portolá Fault at the time of the quake. In 1905 the National Board of Fire Underwriters concluded that the water distribution system was inadequate and faulty and would most likely fail in the event of an emergency.

San Francisco was lucky enough to have a dedicated and visionary fire chief engineer, Dennis Sullivan. Even before the report, he was concerned about the fire department's ability to fight a major citywide fire, catastrophes that had already occurred in Chicago in 1871 and Baltimore in 1904. For years he had warned the city council of the vulnerability of San Francisco to fire. He had proposed that the city badly needed a high-pressure water system, as well as a salt water auxiliary backup. He also proposed identifying and mapping the old cisterns that dotted the city. He had trained and organized an excellent firefighting department, but even the bravest and most skilled can't fight fires without water.

The city council rejected Sullivan's proposals without giving a reason, setting the city up for a spectacular failure.

On the morning of the quake, one of the victims of a building collapse was Chief Sullivan. The chimneys from the hotel next door crashed through the bedrooms in the firehouse. He struggled to get to his wife and fell to the first floor below, where he was scalded by a boiler. Seriously injured, he was carried out by his men.

Instead of Dennis Sullivan, many of the decisions about fighting the massive firestorm were made jointly by General Frederick Funston and Mayor Schmitz. General Funston took charge of the city almost immediately after the quake. He left his house on Sacramento Street and walked to the crown of the hill. He saw the fires beginning and then quickly walked downtown to find the mayor. It was Funston who suggested that the only course open to them was dynamiting buildings in order to create firebreaks — areas of open space wide enough so that the fire could not spread. He took over the strategic dynamiting of much of downtown San Francisco, as well as areas of Nob Hill, Russian Hill, Chinatown, and the east side of Van Ness Avenue.

The process of creating a firebreak by dynamiting buildings has its origin in logic. If the fire has nothing to feed on, it will die. Unfortunately, this process was carried out in many cases by workers who had no experience with explosives. Also, it is necessary to hose down nearby buildings so that they won't catch fire if sparks or chunks of the dynamited building fall on them. In many cases, the fire spread because of the careless use of explosives. People were ordered to leave their homes or businesses even though they were ready to fight to save them.

Some homeowners — such as a valiant and stubborn group on Russian Hill — refused to leave their homes and managed to defeat the fires. Many beautiful homes on the top of the hill were saved — you can still see them today. But most homeowners in the eastern part of the city could not save their homes from the fire, or the dynamite. They had to gather whatever they could carry and then join the stream of refugees heading westward toward the squares and parks out of range of the fire. In survivors' accounts, many mention the eerie quiet, the way the walkers communicated in whispers, and the mournful sound of trunks being dragged through the streets.

The terror of the earthquake was quick — it was over in a little over a minute. The terror of the fire began slowly. Photographs taken that day show people standing about in downtown San Francisco, watching the buildings burn. Oddly, there seems to be no alarm or distress on their faces. There is no blur of panicked movement.

By midday on Wednesday, seven hours after the quake, the fifty or so small fires that had begun with the first shock had leaped and spread into three main fires: the fire south of the Slot, which extended from Market Street to the waterfront; the fire north of Market Street, which encompassed Chinatown, the financial district, and eventually would spread up to Nob Hill and then be halted at

Van Ness; and the "ham and eggs fire" — so named because it was reportedly begun by a woman cooking breakfast with a broken chimney above her stove. This last fire in Hayes Valley would grow and spread with frightening speed, taking out City Hall and then heading for the Mission.

Hospitals were evacuated and the injured moved to the ferries or the Army hospital in the Presidio. The mayor moved his central command three times as again and again the fires took over whole sections of the city.

A firestorm is so powerful that it generates its own wind, which helps to further feed it. In some sections the pavement was so hot it caused people's feet to blister. The superheated air raised the temperatures into the eighties. The smoke cloud rose two miles high over the city.

The firemen of San Francisco faced an impossible task. There were no telephones or fire alarms operating. Messages had to be carried by foot, by car, or by horseback. The fire trucks were pulled by horses. Without functioning hydrants, the firemen had no way to fight the massive blazes. They used everything they had — water from abandoned cisterns, salt water if they could get it, sand, even soda water — to tamp down what they could. They dragged by hand a heavy hose from San Francisco Bay all the way up to Sacramento Street — a trip more than a mile long, and possibly the longest stretch of fire hose in firefighting history, according to historian and former firefighter Dennis Smith. By the time the final firefight took place to hold back the fire at Dolores Street, some of them had been on duty for three days straight. Man and beast fought past the limits of exhaustion.

Personal heroism counted. In two major institutions — the U.S. Mint and the U.S. Post Office — the workers refused to leave. They were brave men who fought the flames with cistern water on the roof of the Mint, and for the post office, with whatever they had on hand. Because of their heroism, after the fire the financial situation in San Francisco remained stable despite the burning of the banks, and the mail continued to be delivered — and nobody had to buy a stamp. For two years, the mail was free.

The writer Jack London, author of *The Call of the Wild*, left his ranch north of the city with his wife, Charmian, shortly after the quake. They traveled as quickly as they could to San Francisco. There he gathered material for his firsthand account of the aftermath of the quake. They walked the city that night until the soles of their feet blistered from the hot sidewalks, and finally slept in a doorway. London later wrote an article for *Collier's Weekly*, telling of the awful beauty of the orange sky and the tremendous wind generated by the firestorm. He told a story of a millionaire on Nob Hill calmly telling him that everything he owned would burn in fifteen minutes and render him penniless.

By the time the fires went out on Saturday, half of the city had been destroyed. Twenty-eight thousand buildings were gone and 225,000 people were homeless. An estimated five hundred city blocks had been incinerated. Whole sections of the city looked as though they'd been wiped out by a massive bomb.

Fire chief Dennis Sullivan did not see or hear of the firestorm that engulfed the city. He never regained consciousness and died of his injuries the fourth day after the earthquake — after the fires had been defeated at last and a cooling rain fell.

City officials worried about investors being scared of rebuilding a city so vulnerable to earthquakes. They set the official death toll at 498, an obvious attempt to convince the world that San Francisco was a safe place to invest. Historians now believe that at least three thousand people perished, and some scholars place the number even higher.

Money and help poured in from around the United States. In a remarkably short period of time, tent cities were set up in Golden Gate Park, the Presidio, and the larger squares. People lined up for food and water. Some people lived in the parks for three years.

The prejudice against the Chinese population that already existed reached a boiling point. Chinatown had been completely destroyed by fire. A plan was set in motion to relocate fourteen thousand Chinese to the mudflats south of the city. Those who fled the city during the fires were prohibited from returning. Racism collided with greed, for it certainly occurred to many that the land Chinatown had taken up was a potentially lucrative parcel close to downtown. It took the personal intervention of the Empress Dowager of China, who declared her intention of rebuilding the Chinese embassy in the heart of where Chinatown had stood, to get the city leaders of the plan to back down.

San Francisco did rebuild, and today it is considered one of the most beautiful cities in the world. But it suffered a blow that took years to recover from. After the quake, industry, commerce, and shipping moved south to Los Angeles.

There are few reminders of the quake today: The hydrant on Church Street that saved the Western Addition is painted gold every April 18. At dawn on April 18, a ceremony is held for Dennis Sullivan, and firefighters dip their ladders in tribute. Five thousand redwood cottages were built to house homeless families after the quake, and two are preserved and can be viewed in the Presidio. The portico of the burned Towne mansion, where

Minnie and her father pause to view the burned-out city, now stands in Golden Gate Park. Called Portals of the Past, it can be found on the shores of Lloyd Lake, a tribute to the courage and perseverance of the people of San Francisco.

At 5:12 in the morning on April 18, 1908, an earthquake tore through San Francisco, destroying huge swaths of the city and killing, contemporary historians believe, more than 3,000 people.

Catastrophic fires billowed throughout the city of San Francisco following the devastating earthquake. Fifty fires began in the first hours after the quake, and joined together to form a wall of flame a mile and a half long.

A crack running down the middle of a San Francisco street indicates the power of the massive 1906 earthquake. Scientists today estimate the quake registered between 7.9 and 8.2 on the Richter scale.

This famous photograph taken by the photographer Arnold Genthe, titled "Looking Down Sacramento Street, San Francisco, April 18, 1906," shows the devastation caused by the earthquake.

After the earthquake, many of the frame houses in San Francisco toppled from their foundations.

Views of Market Street in San Francisco, before the earthquake (above) and after it (below).

After the earthquake, survivors took to the relative safety of the open streets. With half the city destroyed, 225,000 survivors were left homeless. In the photograph on the left, two women are sifting through the rubble of a house, presumably searching for salvageable items. On the right, two men uncover a safe among the rubble and destruction following the earthquake.

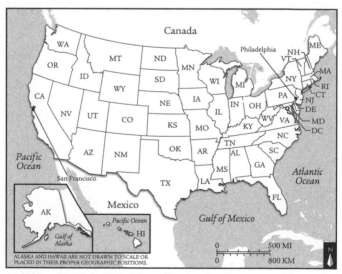

A modern map of the United States showing San Francisco, California, and Philadelphia, Pennsylvania.

AUTHOR'S NOTE

On writing *A City Tossed and Broken*, author Judy Blundell noted, "I was lucky enough to live in San Francisco twice in my life, and it remains one of my favorite cities. On my walks from my apartment in Noe Valley to Dolores Park (called Mission Park in Minnie's time), I always made sure to walk on the side of the street where the golden hydrant commemorated the last great battle to douse the Mission District fire. I often stopped to read the plaque. That spot offers a grand vista overlooking the city, and I would stand for a moment and try to imagine what it all looked like in 1906.

"I experienced several quakes while living in the city, but nothing like the event of 1906. I do remember the feeling of surprise when the shaking begins — and the spurt of fear every San Franciscan feels when they think, *Is this the big one?* In researching this book I soon learned that the earthquake and subsequent firestorm were much worse than even my imagination had conjured up those years ago. The three days after the quake were not as simple as I'd thought — history rarely is. Wrong decisions and blunders were made, some took advantage of the calamity, but by and large the citizens of San Francisco showed remarkable courage and optimism during and after the ordeal. I think Minnie has the same character traits that led so many to make San Francisco their home—an adventurous spirit and a talent for reinvention."

Judy also encourages anyone who wants to know more about the quake to read the fascinating personal accounts of those who lived through it. They are available online at the Virtual Museum of the City of San Francisco: www.sfmuseum.org/1906/ew.html.

Judy Blundell is the National Book Award–winning author of *What I Saw and How I Lied* and the acclaimed novel *Strings Attached*. In addition, she has written many other books for middle-grade and young-adult readers under various pseudonyms, including a host of Star Wars novels; *Premonitions*, which was an ALA Reluctant Readers Best Picks and was chosen by the New York Public Library as a 2004 Best Books for the Teen Age; and *Beyond the Grave* (Book 4), *In Too Deep* (Book 6), *Vespers Rising* (Book 11), and *A King's Ransom* (Book 2 of Cahills vs. Vespers) for the *New York Times* bestselling series The 39 Clues, as Jude Watson. Judy lives in Katonah, New York, with her family.

ACKNOWLEDGMENTS

Grateful acknowledgment is made for permission to use the following:

Cover portrait by Tim O'Brien.

Cover background: City Hall, April 1906, San Francisco, Library of Congress.

Page 214: Man walking up a devastated San Francisco street, ibid.

Page 215 (top): Catastrophic fires billowing through San Francisco following the devastating earthquake, ibid.

Page 215 (bottom): A crack running down the middle of a San Francisco street, ibid.

Page 216 (top): "Looking Down Sacramento Street, San Francisco, April 18, 1906," by photographer Arnold Genthe, ibid.

Page 216 (bottom): San Francisco houses toppling from their foundations, ibid.

Page 217 (top): San Francisco's Market Street before the earthquake, ibid.

Page 217 (bottom): San Francisco's Market Street after the earthquake, ibid.

Page 218 (top left): Two women survivors sifting through the rubble of a house, ibid.

Page 218 (top right): Two men survivors uncovering a safe among the rubble and destruction, ibid.

Page 218 (bottom): Map by Jim McMahon.

OTHER BOOKS IN
THE DEAR AMERICA SERIES

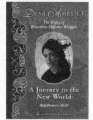

Available in print and e-book editions.